She Feeds on Misery

Emily Vale

Emily Vale Books

Cover Art: Canva, Emily Vale

Editor: Earley Editing LLC

ISBN paperback: 979-8-9931879-0-7

ISBN ebook: 979-8-9931879-1-4

Contents

Content Warnings

Dear Reader, below is a list of subject matter that may be viewed as sensitive to some. While this is a light-hearted Horror with comedic elements that's injected with more ridiculous moments rather than overly gruesome ones, Sasha's still in the misery business. I view it as my duty to prepare readers for anything that may be emotionally triggering. Happy reading!

- Reference of sexual assault (No descriptions)

- Reference to infidelity

- Hamster sacrifice (No torture or graphic detail)

- Murder by induced overdose (Needle Involved)

- Religious themes (Demonic Entity)

Dedication

We all have demons to face and baggage to unpack.

Let's go on a girl's trip.

SFOM Playlist

Scan a QR code to listen

SPOTIFY

Chapter 1

Escape

"Leave It All Behind for Turquoise Seas and Spectacular Coastlines," reads a magazine title for the world's best beaches. If only that's where this plane was headed.

I flip through the glossy pages while the flight attendant approaches with her beverage cart. It gently rolls and then stops with a click at every seat. No surprise, Australia makes the pick. Maybe, in another life, we would have made it there. I take a photo of it to show Maven later.

She'll be the one good part of this trip, a light in the storm. We've been through it all, and no matter what we've always been there for each other when others weren't. When we were younger, we dreamed of making it there for a fantasy summer beach escape, Australia. We'd talk about staying in a beach bungalow, get surfer boyfriends, and swim nude in a warm, crystalline ocean—that was before she got pregnant.

It's turned into a running joke. *"Meet me at the beach. No biki-nis."* At least, I view it as a joke now. A lot changed after we were forced to grow up, but we never forgot about our dream.

I pull the window shade down, tuck the magazine back into its compartment, and settle into my seat after reclining it back all two inches. I'm a pro at this, honestly: sleeping during a flight. I take my silk sleep mask out of my bag, along with my neck pillow, just in time for the beverage cart to reach my row.

"Anything to drink, miss?"

"Do you have any vodka?"

"We sure do." She winks. "Be right back."

It's only a two-and-a-half-hour flight from New York to Atlanta, but I really do need that drink if I'm going to make it through my yearly obligatory trip home. Plus, an older man is next to me snoring already—roaring past the hum of the engines.

I put my earbuds in while a part of me wonders why I still visit when I can only stand my parents in short increments. One week each year always seems too long and too short of a visit at the same time. I suppose I still make these trips, mostly, to see my best friend, even if we only tend to hang out for fewer days than we'd both like.

Not this time, though.

I finally pulled Maven's leg hard enough, so we're going on our first girl's trip—one that's majorly overdue. No matter how much time passes or how unrelatable we become to each other, the connection never fades. Time rewinds when we get together. Beneath our daily routines and the exterior, we know each other on soul level. No one else knows me the way she does, and no one else outside of my family has known me for *as long* as she has.

I think they say if a friendship lasts seven years, then it's supposed to last forever. We're going on twenty-two years of friendship, though

more than half of that has been long distance. After college, I moved to
New York and never looked back. Every person in my life now, besides
her, is either a co-worker or a casual friend. We'll meet up for dinner
or at the bar; we have a good time and don't ask each other too many
personal questions. I'm okay with that; it's easy.

The attendant brings me my drink, and I sing her praises. "Mmm.
Thank you."

Taking advantage of the in-flight Wi-Fi, I check some emails before
I officially clock out for my vacation. I can't seem to get away from
work. I'll admit it's an addiction. It's what I'm good at, and not only
does it pay the bills but it allows me to afford my lifestyle. I enjoy my
work as a data scientist enough, or as much as anyone could enjoy a
job, I guess.

Then, with the act of turning my phone to airplane mode, I'm
officially signing off for the next week. I pull up Spotify, finish my
drink in record time, and drag my silk sleeping mask down—a sign for
no one to talk to me until we get there.

The first few days with my parents went by surprisingly smoothly. I
managed to avoid too much time around my father and timed it just
right so I wouldn't be spending a Sunday here, where Mom would
inevitably guilt me into going to church with her. I don't really rock
with organized religion anymore, but she makes sure to let me know
she prays for me every night.

"Thanks, Mom," I tell her, as I pull the zipper closed on my suitcase.

I believe in something bigger, but in my experience, half the people in the congregation are hypocrites anyway. I'd rather believe what I believe and not have to prove it to anyone. I know firsthand there are people who show up and play the part, but then are the complete opposite behind closed doors. Some of the most godly presenting are the most wicked. What I believe is between me and whatever god there is.

"Do you really need all this space?" Mom asks.

I load my suitcase into the back of the white Jeep Wagoneer I rented. I told Dad bye inside, but Mom followed me out to send me off.

I move the sticky hair off my forehead. "No, but it was a better option than the Prius."

It's a ridiculously hot September in Atlanta, and I doubt I'll get any reprieve from the heat where I'm headed.

She smooths out my hair, which is waving from the spike of humidity, then she gently grips my shoulders. "You're so pretty, Blair. I really wish you would settle down and find a good Christian man."

I smile back at her. "Maybe," while really thinking, *Not a chance*.

It's not the first time I've heard this wish of hers, and it won't be the last either. She'll keep saying it until she realizes it's too late for me. At thirty-six, there's still time, but I think it's pretty clear I have no intention of settling down. I'm not the first working woman to think this way either. There are many women I know who have lives outside of a man. I don't *need* one, I do just fine by myself. I enjoy my freedom, not having to answer to someone when you want to make a purchase or stay out late. Random hookups have served me just fine. I don't *have* to get to know them and they don't *have* to get to know me. I keep it light, keep it fun, non committal. It's best that way.

"Well, I'm off to Maven's." I press the button, closing the hatch. "Love you, Mom."

"Love you too, honey." Her lips tighten. "You know I don't like that city, but all I can ask is that you be safe." She kisses me on the cheek.

"I'm always safe," I say, gripping the keys in my hand. "We'll be fine."

I knock three times on the large wooden door with a fanciful wreath hanging on it, made with rows of eucalyptus and lavender. I wouldn't be surprised if she made it herself, she's always been good at stuff like that. Maven swings it open with an ecstatic smile stretched across her face.

"Long time, no see," I say with a grin.

She envelops me in a hug. "Ah! I missed you."

"Missed you more," I say. "Ready for the trip of a lifetime?"

"You know I am." Wearing a white cropped sweater over a casual sky-blue maxi dress, she looks effortlessly pretty. Unlike her, I have to put in the effort. Thank God for winged eyeliner. "Come in," she encourages, opening the door wider. "I have to grab my bags from the bedroom. Be right back."

I stand in the quiet entry-way, surrounded by professional black-and-white family photos. Being able to see Junior grow up from photo to photo—from his toothless grin, to a snaggle-toothed boy, to a grown man—makes me smile. Mave and Matt made a cute kid, though I always thought she could do way better than her husband, but I digress.

Maven returns, dragging out more suitcases than she needs for a few days. I grab one to help her load them all into the vehicle.

"We're only staying there for three days. How much stuff are you bringing?" I ask, rolling the suitcase out to the driveway.

"I need choices. And when did you cut your hair? It looks chic."

"Chic? I'll take it. A few months ago."

I decided to make the big chop after I saw some girl walking the streets of Manhattan with a French bob and thought, *You know what, I need something new.*

"Where's Matt?" I ask, not because I care about the comings and goings of the man himself, but it seems proper to acknowledge his existence.

"Oh he's out golfing." She tosses the last bag into the back. "I'm driving by the way."

"I won't argue with that. You know I hate driving." One of the luxuries of living in New York City is that I'm at the mercy of cab drivers and the subway. "Do you think the street cars cover the whole city?"

"Don't know. Where are we staying?" she asks.

"The Garden District. I found this really cool Airbnb—you'll like it."

I didn't have to search for the perfect stay for very long. The pink shotgun house with shutters painted teal caught my eye immediately, with a listing that read: *Enjoy an unforgettable stay in the historic Garden District of New Orleans. This hauntingly beautiful home is loaded with charm and in an ideal central location, offering adventure at your fingertips. It will be a great escape for you to relax and enjoy your stay in Crescent City. Beware of the ghosts and don't go in the attic unless you dare.*

Maven has a thing for aesthetics. I like nice things too, but I wanted to make sure I picked a cute place for such a special trip. Her house is a testament of her devotion to appearances, though a lot more tame than the house before us. It's a girl's trip after all, so why not book a pink house?

I get into the passenger seat, looking out at her flower-beds which are just as immaculate as they were last year. Everything she has is taken care of and has its place. That woman never misses a beat, and I don't know how she does it.

When it comes to herself in particular, Maven's long and wavy, golden blonde hair is consistently highlighted, and she takes care of Matt better than she should. I feel like I can barely keep up with my own needs some days, while she keeps up this house like it's due to be on a *Better Homes and Gardens* ad.

Without any time to waste, I give Maven the address for our stay and we set off to our destination.

"Road trip!" I call out. "I curated a playlist just for this, I hope you know."

"I wouldn't expect anything less."

When I had my first serious boyfriend in high school, I burned a CD and gave it to him. It was a casual composition with music like *Suga Suga* by Baby Bash. I try to erase it from my memory. I made a similar playlist for when Maven and Matt got married at seventeen, just after high school graduation. I haven't curated a wedding playlist since. The actual adults didn't appreciate *It's Goin' Down*, by Yung Joc as much as Maven and I did. Junior was one at the time, at least he liked it and we have something to laugh about to this day.

"What's Junior up to these days?" I ask, as we merge onto the busy interstate.

"Oh he's off living his best life at Duke. I really don't see him much anymore. Can you believe he turns twenty-one this year?"

"God. No. When I think of him, I can still picture him eating his own boogers."

She laughs. "Me too, sometimes."

"Oh. I have something to show you. I saw this on the flight here." I pull up the photo of the magazine article listing all the best shimmering beaches to escape life's problems. "There's still time for us to abandon everything."

She sighs. "Ah, one day. I really missed you, B."

"I missed you too," I say, with a familiar comfort spreading through my chest.

Chapter 2

Nest

Driving through the forested back roads of Mississippi, we've cycled through the carefully curated playlist. Nothing but green landscapes pass by. There's been an occasional sign, some seemingly vacant homes, and one decrepit church over the past hour. With weeds and vines and trees taking over, I question Maven's navigation skills.

"Are you sure this is the quickest way?" I pull up the GPS on my phone, but it doesn't load beyond a blank, gray screen.

"Yeah. It's what the map said." She leisurely grips the steering wheel, sunglasses propped on top of her head. "What? Have you spent so much time in the big city that it unnerves you to be too far away from the hustle and bustle?"

"No. I'm more concerned about taking a wrong turn and being forced to go to a gas station that's operated by cannibals."

She looks at me unenthused. "Everyone knows those gas stations are in West Virginia, not Mississippi."

"Look." I point to an empty and rusted pickup truck parked in the grass at the end of the short bridge we're going over. "Evidence."

She rolls her eyes then lowers her shades. "We do need gas though. Next station, we're stopping—despite your hate of the countryside."

"I'll deal."

She changes the subject. "So...what ever happened to Isabel? It seemed like it was getting serious. I thought surely I would meet one of your significant others by now."

"I don't know."

"Don't do that. Of course you know. What happened?"

I look up. "The same thing that always happens. Me. She wanted to move in and I told her I wasn't comfortable with that."

"Why not?" She prods.

I wiggle in my seat. "I like my independence."

"And that's more important to you than having someone you care about around?" I don't answer for a minute because I'm trying to figure out how to. "And it's okay if it is," Maven reassures me.

"I guess it is."

That's how the story goes every time. It's how it went with Dillon, who was the nicest person I've ever been with, but maybe too nice for me. Either way, I ruined it because I couldn't give him what he deserved. It's how it went with Ben when he told me, *"You just... feel temporary."* That fucking hurt to hear. And it's clearly how it went with Isabel.

The only person I ever moved in with was about ten years ago. Liam was also my longest relationship—at four years. I tried my hardest to be a relationship girl for him, I wanted to be so badly, more than I should have because it turns out near the end he was cheating on me. Even though it's totally against every feminist bone in my body, I still kind of think I drove him to it. I sabotaged myself at every point, without understanding why still to this day.

It's just not in my nature to let someone love me too much or I'm just not good at commitment. It is what it is.

I look out the window, into a deep ravine where I can see nothing but growth as my mind wanders. We listen to a true crime podcast to fill the void of time and silence and I go in and out of paying attention to it. They're recounting a story about a Black Widow who traveled the country under different aliases, finding rich men to fall in love with her, only to collect on their life insurance later.

Why do I let my romantic relationships self-destruct before they can evolve into something further? I feel like I know the answer, it's there somewhere, but I'm protecting myself by not introspecting on it for long enough. At least I'm not living a lie, like the Black Widow, pretending to love someone for selfish benefit. I'm not doing it for my benefit, no. It's just how I am.

Twenty minutes later, we arrive at a gas station that's not utterly hopeless. It's probably one of those where I'll squint my eyes when I go to the bathroom just to make sure I don't see the pee-stained tiles or soggy toilet paper on the floor too clearly. Maven pumps the gas while I go inside to use the bathroom and stock up on road food.

There's a faint buzzing as I approach the door to the gas station. Just as I grab for the handle, something brown settles above my wrist and a sudden prick of pain stabs me. "Fuck!"

I snatch my hand from the door and press my arm into my body. It happened so fast I didn't see the winged insect clearly enough. To my luck, I'm not allergic to any of their stings. Still, it hurts. I look down at the tiny red spot above my wrist that will begin to swell.

I come back to the vehicle with beef jerky, Benadryl, drinks, and gum—to replace the cigarettes which I'm trying to kick.

"What's up with the antihistamine?" Maven questions.

"A bee or one of its cousins stung me."

"The weirdest things always seem to happen to you."

I take two capsules from their foils and pop them in my mouth, drinking them down with some water. "I know."

After six-and-a-half hours, several gas station snacks, and one energy drink later, we pull up to our rental. I retrieve the code the host gave me, standing on the steps of the cute pink house. The teal shutters and floor-to-ceiling windows give away that it's been renovated from the original design. Ornate white trim encapsulates the small porch that's been added—it's totally what I imagined when I thought of staying here in New Orleans. Despite the bright paint job, I can tell there's loads of history in every splinter of wood. I'm curious what kind of person paints their house pink and teal or if it was done purely for the intent of attracting vacationers.

"Great job, B. This place is adorable." Maven awes at the curb appeal.

"Right? It's perfect for us."

I type in the code on the keypad and the lock turns with a shifting sound. Opening the door, the inside is just as cute as the outside. An original, though non-functional, brick fireplace centers the living room. There's clean, modern furnishings, fresh flowers, and even some muffins on the kitchen counter-top. They're store bought, but I don't discriminate. I don't think I've had a bad muffin in my life.

We walk down the length of the home, in search of the bedroom. There are two queen mattresses, a connected bathroom, and a large vanity inside. I throw my suitcase onto the bed closest to the door.

"I'm pretty tired from the drive. Start our day tomorrow?" Maven suggests, as she utilizes one of the luggage racks.

I kick my shoes off. "Yeah I'd have to agree. I'll order us some food and we can have a signature Maven and Blair movie night. How about that?"

"That sounds like a dream. I'm going to take a shower. I'll just take a salad from wherever, please and thank you." She grabs her toiletry bag and heads for the bathroom.

I change into an over-sized vintage band tee and over-the-knee striped socks. Plopping onto the bed, I channel surf while waiting for her to come out of the shower. Thirty minutes later, I inhale the food we had delivered while we sit in bed after finally deciding on *Buffy the Vampire Slayer*.

"I don't think I've ever eaten anything this good before," I say around a mouthful.

She got a healthier option—a cobb salad. "It sure smells amazing," she says.

News to me is she went vegan in the past year.

"Since when did you make that switch?" I ask. We used to update each other on everything, no matter how minor.

"Well, Matt got really into fitness about a year ago. And I *do* feel better since making the switch. It's not so bad when you get used to it."

"I never want to describe my food as *not so bad*." I take a long gulp of my sweet tea. They just don't make it like this in New York. "Are you sure you don't want to have a taste?" I wave my crawfish bread in front of her.

"I'm sure, but thanks for the offer."

We huddle in bed and finish the episode. "I'm oddly not even tired anymore," I admit.

"Me either. And that's weird, because I usually go to bed by nine-thirty."

"Excuse me? You're not elderly." She pushes my shoulder, throwing me off balance, making the sting above my wrist throb ever so faintly.

"I get tired. I do a lot."

"I know you do," I tell her.

Besides being the kick-ass homemaker she is, she's also a successful business owner. She went viral on TikTok for making sourdough loaves and now sells sourdough starters, recipes, and kits to people who want to follow in her footsteps. She's always been likable. I'm not so much. I'm like the opposite of likable. I think the younger generation would call us a black cat and golden retriever.

"If we're not sleeping, want to be nosey?" I suggest, raising my brows.

"Hmm." She thinks. "Sure. Let's go investigate."

We look through the bedroom and hall closets to disappointingly find there's not much besides a clothing iron, linens, and cleaning supplies. "Well this is boring," I say. I was hoping to come across a secret stash of goodies or a door that was accidentally left unlocked.

Maven's gaze jumps above us. "There's an attic. I saw the window outside."

I follow her line of sight. "Huh. You're right. I thought that was a joke."

"Thought what was a joke?"

"Oh. The listing. It said not to go in the attic because of the ghosts."

She crosses her arms. "That would have been valuable knowledge. Did you book us a haunted house?"

I shrug as I reach for the cord. "Maybe."

She puts her hand on my arm. "Wait what if their belongings are up there?"

With a confused look on my face, "Yeah so what. Are you chickening out?"

"No," she says, straightening her posture. "Just a sec, I'll be right back." She jogs back a few seconds later, wearing furry white slippers. "You should wear shoes too. No telling what animals have been up there."

"My socks will protect me. Let's go ghost hunting."

She waves her hand. "I'm not entertaining that."

I pull the cord, meeting some resistance, though revealing a ladder I have to unfold. A thick odor of dust, wood, and something else kind of sour and sweet comes trailing out. I cough. "Do you really still think I'm lying about that?"

When I first moved to the city, I was in a shitty apartment and it was old as dirt. It had ghosts to match, too. Upon further investigation, all of my neighbors had experienced something of the sort as well. One morning I woke up to a woman wearing a long white dress at the foot of my bed. I could see straight through her. Maven was the first person I called and she asked me how much I drank the night before. It's not that big of a deal, but it really happened and it appears she's still unsure of my testimony.

"I've never lied a day in my life," I say, keeping it light.

"*Okayyy.* No, I believe you saw what you saw. I just don't believe you've never lied a day in your life."

"Okay. I've never lied—to you." I climb up the ladder, using the flashlight on my phone. I stand up fully in the dimly lit attic space as she follows behind. "Holy shit, this is bigger than I thought."

The attic spans the entire square footage of the home. It's big enough to do something with. Thick wooden beams run across the slope of the roof, coming to a peak.

Maven stands beside me. "It makes me think of the attic in *Charmed*. It would be so cute if they fixed this up and made it into another bedroom or an entertainment room. It's wasted potential." I just know she's dreaming up the floor plan in her head.

The contents are mostly storage boxes, filled with what appears to be seasonal decor. *How much seasonal decor does one person need?* There's plastic cases filled with Mardi Gras beads, Halloween yard decor, an artificial Christmas tree, and Easter eggs—it's a holiday warehouse. I almost wish we were staying here closer to a holiday so I could see what it all looks like on display.

We head to the front of the attic where the crammed boxes open to an emptied space. There's a window with a sliver of moonlight shining through and illuminating the dusty floor boards.

"What's that on the floor?" Maven asks.

I come closer into the beams the moon provides. "It's a Ouija board!"

"Oh. No. No, no, no, no, no." She raises her hands, shaking her head.

"Oh. Come on, don't be so superstitious. Aren't you the one that has a hard time believing in ghosts?"

"I never said that." She holds her hand to her chest looking fake offended.

I stick out my bottom lip in a pout. "They probably put this here as a prop. Look, it's brand new." I crouch down, touching the pristine cardboard. "There's not even any dust on it."

"If something haunts my dreams, I blame you."

"They're just feeding into the theme of the city. Nothing is going to haunt your dreams." I smile, barely containing my excitement.

The old wooden planks of the floor creak beneath our weight as we sit crisscross. Conveniently next to the board, the planchet sits in wait. With the bright moon moving through the attic, it's the perfect atmosphere for something slightly spooky.

I crane my head up to see spiders spinning in the beams, hoping one doesn't suspend downward. I squint my eyes at a small dark mass gathered in the corner of the main support beam. Shining my light on it, I find a hornet's nest. An empty one, thank goodness.

Not like I needed to add to the creepy and potentially infested ambiance, I turn off my flashlight to set the mood anyway.

"Have you ever played this before?" Maven asks.

"Nope. You're popping my spirit board cherry."

This board looks like every other one you see in the stores, a tan board with black Gothic lettering. There's a sun in the upper corner with the word *yes* and a moon on the other side with the word *no*. Likewise, there's a *hello* and *goodbye* in the bottom corners.

"Wow. I didn't know you still had any cherries left to be popped," Maven adds.

I give her the middle finger, then hover the planchet over the board. "I think you have to put two fingers from both hands lightly on the thing," I say.

"Okay. Fingers are on the thing," Maven declares.

She places her perfectly French tipped manicured nails on top of it and I do the same, except mine are merely clean with no adornments. We sit there for about ten seconds, staring at the board, fingers still.

"This feels stupid," she whispers.

"Give it a minute." Filling the empty space and empty activity, I shimmy my shoulders. "Does it make you feel young again?"

"No. And thank God. When I was a teenager I was stressed out and changing diapers."

"Right," I say.

"But being with you, doing something stupid does make me feel—" Her sentence is cut off by the subtle movement beneath our fingertips. "Are you moving it?" she whispers.

"No."

"Stop lying. You're moving it."

"I'm not fucking moving it, I swear."

The planchet slowly glides down and left, landing on the word *Hello.*

"Hello," I say, more as a question. The air suddenly feels chillier. The insulation must be lackluster up here.

"I always wondered how these things worked. There must be some magnet inside," Maven says.

"Inside the cardboard?"

"I'm sure they found a way."

Goose bumps form on my arm, but I've committed to this. "So should we ask it something?"

"Like what?"

"Who are you?" I question.

It slowly moves over to the letter *S.*

Maven and I lock eyes, suggesting neither of us are moving it. The planchet pulls away from me, floating like it's on ice and increasing speed with each letter. "A, S, H, A."

"Sasha? Nice to meet you," Maven says through gritted teeth.

"Is this freaking you out?" I ask. Now that something is actually happening, I wouldn't blame her for wanting to call it quits.

"No. It's fine. It's just a magic trick, right?"

"Yeah," I say. "Hah. Magnets, I guess." *Hell if I know.*

I mean, it could be real. I know the woman I saw in my room was real. I know I haven't given it as much thought as I probably should have before this moment because not everyone lives to see an apparition in a fully awake state. That one guy from the ghost hunting show for example saw one and made it his whole personality—his life's mission. I saw one and pretended I didn't.

Maybe other people witness things too and we just don't know because no one talks about it. Because it sounds crazy right? Like believing this thing is actually moving by itself, not a result of magnetism or another person pulling a prank. Believing that would be insane.

"Are you friendly?" I ask the board.

It floats to *yes*.

"What else should we ask it?" asks Maven. I shrug. "Are you...deceased?" The planchet slowly glides to *no*. "Hmm," she sounds.

"Then, what are you?" I ask.

The chill in the air becomes heavier. There's a creak. We turn our heads to the source, the cracked open window that I don't remember being open before.

"Is this a good idea?" Maven asks.

"It's only cardboard."

The planchet suddenly moves to the letters, *D, E, M*.

"Hell, no." Maven shoots up. "I don't care if this is cardboard, I'm not playing around with the idea of that.

"Want to call it a night, then? Sorry we're not too entertaining, Sasha." I chuckle.

"Not funny," Maven comments.

I am rightfully a little freaked, but I won't admit it. I can't quite decide for myself if it is only cardboard and magnetism or something more. Either way, I'll take Maven's lead on closing this out. Maven gets up and dusts off her light pink matching pajama set.

"Aren't we supposed to like say goodbye first?" I ask.

"You're asking the wrong person."

Whatever. It's not real. I dust off my legs. "These socks are definitely embedded with spider webs and rat poop."

"Should have worn shoes."

We both stand up, headed for the hatch door in the unfamiliar dark attic. "Where's your flashlight?" she asks. "I can barely see anything."

I search for my phone on the wooden floorboard, bent over, and grazing my hands across the dusty layer. When I find it, I turn on my light. We freeze because as soon as I turn on my flashlight, all other light seems to leave the room. The moonlight is blocked out.

"Maybe it's cloudy," I offer. I can tell Maven's spooked because she grabs my hand and we walk back to the ladder together. "You go first," I tell her.

She wades through the aisle of storage containers while I glance at the small window where the light was coming in, where it should be still. That's when I see it, a shadow, dark and foreboding.

Once she goes down, I lower my leg, making contact with the first step, but unable to peel my eyes away. I reduce my chance of making any noise by moving slowly, though if there's another person in here that tactic is obsolete because they know I'm here—it just seems like being quiet is the right thing to do in uncertain terms. I question if it's a trick of the eye, my own anxiety or a play of light. The blackness occupies the far wall, frozen, like it knows I'm watching. Surely it's watching me in return if it has eyes somewhere among the blackness. Maybe it does, but they're so dark they blend in with the rest. I watch it shrink, the black mass becoming denser as it reduces in size. The window is now partially blocked by a human-sized void and the moon creeps back in, disproving my earlier and hopeful theory of clouds blocking the moon. I can't believe my eyes, so I won't.

Fuck this.

My chest rises and falls as I climb down the ladder, moving frantically to fold the contraption back up, my wrist throbbing from the sting as I do so. The attic door closes with a loud *thud.* Maven is standing there with a confused and concerned look on her face.

"You okay?" she asks.

"Yeah. I thought I saw another hornet," I lie.

Don't go in the attic, the listing said. Maybe I should have heeded that advice.

Chapter 3

Starving

I crack open my eyes to the sounds of water running in the bathroom. My cheek feels wet. I lift my head off the pillow and wipe the back of my hand across it, removing the drool. I slept like the dead, while simultaneously having the weirdest dream I can't quite remember.

It was more of a lingering presence in my memory rather than an actual recollection of a dream, an empty feeling. My consciousness was stuck in a dark recess of my mind where I was accompanied by utter hopelessness. It's been a while since I've had a nightmare, if you could even call it that.

I blink my eyes a few times, thankful for this plane of existence and drop my legs over the side of the bed, my bare feet contacting the cold floor and waking me up a little bit more. I drag myself to the bathroom, where I join Maven at the double sink.

"Sleep well?" she asks.

"You could say that." I feel well rested, but I sure don't look it. My reflection reveals I sweated through my t-shirt. Gross. "Did you have any weird dreams last night?"

She pats her mouth dry, wearing a dusty-rose satin robe. "No. If I did, I don't remember it. Why, did you?"

"Kind of. I've had weirder ones, though. I'm gonna hop in the shower."

I'm feeling better after a full body scrub down. This host went one step further, supplying not just the regular fixings like body wash and shampoo, but a body scrub that smells like cherries. I do my morning ritual of putting in my contacts then my skincare routine consisting of a bougie antioxidant serum my esthetician recommended and SPF. I step out of the bathroom in my towel to see Maven already putting on her makeup.

"Any agenda for today?" she asks.

I planned most everything for this trip, besides Maven's one must, a stop at a historic perfumery. She has a couple of things she nerds out about, which include perfume—that's been an always thing. Plants are a more recent fixation, but she's got a hell of a green thumb for a beginner if her flower-beds have anything to show for it.

"The cooking class I told you about is today around noon. We'll actually be"—I swat a fly away—"cooking each other's lunch."

I'm excited to learn some new things. I just hope I don't disappoint by over-cooking or skipping an ingredient as I admittedly don't do much cooking for one. I open my suitcase, still hearing the awful buzzing while trying to ignore it. I opt for a denim halter top that grazes my hips and low-rise black pants. It'll be warm in the kitchen and black pants don't stain.

"Cute!" Maven says, from the vanity she's perched at across the room.

Something that hasn't changed is she always asks what I'm wearing first, so she can match her outfit to a similar aesthetic. It's not like she needs any kind of style direction, she's known to have five minutes to get dressed and step out like she's had the outfit prepped the night before. It's kind of like that cute married couple you see always wearing coordinating colors, it's just the way we function. It occurs to me that's why she over-packed.

She pulls out a short sleeved denim jumpsuit and sheds her robe. It hugs her body and flares at the leg.

"Where'd you get that? I want one."

She beams. "I'll get you one for Christmas."

"I wouldn't be mad. I'm a size four by the way."

"Like I don't know. We've been the same size since eighth grade."

I sit on the bed with my makeup bag, spotting on some concealer in the areas where I need it, then locking it in with a little loose powder followed by a deep pink shade of blush and expertly applied winged eyeliner. I've been doing the same look since I was in my twenties.

Maven's done before I am, so she sits across from me on her bed. The buzzing returns. I spot the fly going around the room in a chaotic pattern before it lands on my makeup bag. I swat for it and miss. This house definitely needs to be sprayed for bugs.

"So how's work been?" Maven asks to fill the silence. "We never talk about your work."

I scan the room one last time before giving up and returning to the task at hand, applying some mascara. So long as a fly doesn't buzz around my head, I shouldn't poke my eye out. "The work of a data scientist is not much to talk about, but good."

"Good? No juicy gossip? I think you're holding back on me. Come on, I know you have something. I make bread and record videos all day. I'm the one who's boring."

I drop my mascara wand. "You're never boring." It's true to me, even if she doesn't think so. "Well I do have one thing, sort of the reason I really wanted to take this trip."

"Yeah?"

"I uh got a new position. It's not in New York, though. It's in London."

"London? Wow. That's amazing, that's...a big change." She presses her lips together.

I wait for her to say what's on her mind, but she stays silent.

"Yeah," I go on, "it's a big change. It pays better and I think it's time for new scenery anyways. New York is home, but it still doesn't feel permanent. You know? I thought I'd give London a chance."

She fidgets with the decorative ruffle on the comforter. "I can't imagine picking up and moving to Europe. I wouldn't know what to do with myself."

I shrug. "I'm not sure I do know what I'm doing, but I've got to do something so it may as well be exciting."

"I wonder what the time difference is?"

"Five hours. I looked it up," I offer.

"That's not so bad, I guess."

The reason I wanted to take this trip is because I'm not sure when I'll be back, but I won't tell her that so plainly.

"This new position is busier. It's just a new direction, so I'm not sure how often I'll be visiting once I get settled there."

She takes a moment, still pressing her lips together. "Maybe I could visit you, then."

The corners of my mouth lift into a smile. "You could."

In all the time I've been away, she's never come to see me, no one has. Yeah, I'm the one who moved away but I haven't forgotten about anyone. I dutifully come back year after year. But I don't put that on Maven. She built a life where she's raising a family.

The suggestion of her coming to visit makes me smile, though my smile quickly dissipates. Somehow I know it to only be a suggestion that will go unfulfilled.

Maven pops her knuckles nervously. "You know Matt doesn't like me to travel without him, but forget that. Really, I'll come see you."

I smile. "I know you would."

I need something different. Life has gotten...stale. As much as it hurts to accept this departure from what I've made routine, I need to do what's best for me. I don't know what that entails, but I'm sure I'll discover that as I go.

I put on deodorant and check myself out in the full-length mirror. Behind me in the reflection, I see her looking at her phone. Maven releases a heavy sigh.

"What's that about?"

"I checked in with Matt and he didn't water my plants yesterday evening like he said he would." She closes her eyes and lets out a resetting breath.

"So. What's wrong with skipping a day?"

"If he didn't do it then, he's not going to do it at all and I'm going to come back to wilted flowers." She presses her fingers to her forehead.

"Why do you care so much? It's only a few days. I'm sure they'll be fine."

"It's not illegal to care about things, Blair."

"Ouch. Okay are we arguing about plants?"

She drops her shoulders. "No. We're not arguing about plants." She walks over and puts her arms around me, in a tight hug. "Let's go get breakfast, huh?"

Just as quickly as her disappointment arrived from the failed promise her husband made, she was able to extinguish it.

"Breakfast sounds good," I say.

We step out into the hallway and hear a clatter happening in the kitchen. We both freeze.

Maven grips my shoulder. "What the hell was that?"

The noise—it's not something falling off the wall, it sounds like someone is rifling through the cabinets. An intruder. We back into the doorway.

"Someone's in there," I whisper to Maven, peering my head out to listen. "Do you have your phone?" She reaches into her pocket and holds up her cell. "Dial 9-1-1!" I plead as quietly as possible.

"I wouldn't do that," a playful female voice calls from the kitchen.

I grab Maven's arm and pull her farther into the bedroom, shutting the door and locking it with lightning speed. We rush to the bed, crouching on it like scared children as if it will protect us, too.

"Who the fuck are you?" I yell out. "Get out now, I'm calling the police!" Maven still has the phone in her hand with a paralyzed look on her face. "What are you doing, call the cops!" I urge her.

She looks like she's seen a ghost. Has this happened to her before? An intruder? Why isn't she doing anything? She's frozen. This must be what PTSD looks like in some cases. She's not even looking at me. She's looking through me, past me...behind me. Her frozen face contorts into an expression of ultimate terror.

"Blair!" she yells out to whatever's behind me.

I don't want to look behind me, but I have to. I join Maven's chorus of terror when I see a woman who is casually leaning against the bathroom doorframe.

That's the most terrifying part—the shock of her being in the bedroom with us, not her. She's not horribly terrifying in appearance, per say, but I still fix my gaze on her, anticipating whatever comes next. Her wispy jet-black hair rests at her hips. She has long slender limbs and pale skin, but is striking in an odd way, kind of like a strange fairy in a dark fairy tale.

While holding a muffin in each hand, she crams them into her mouth like a wild animal. I tilt my head, failing to understand her motives. She's broken into the house, is double-fisting our muffins, and is standing in our room. I don't care to theorize how she got in here through a locked door. I'm more concerned with us getting out.

I pounce off the bed and grab the closest thing to me, a small lamp. "Who are you and why the hell are you in our room?"

She's not fazed by how unsettled we are that she's broken into our rental. She stands confidently wearing all black, leather leggings, black peep toed boots and a black tank top. And she's still eating the damn pastry.

"You can call me Sasha," she says around the crumbs as she shrugs. "I go by many names, but I've been liking that one lately."

I grip the lamp a little tighter. "Maven, do the thing."

This woman is likely certifiably insane. She had to be the one in the attic last night. I'm not sure how she messed with the Ouija board, but I'm now convinced she did and that it was her I saw putting on some shadow show.

Maven trembles, gripping at my arm from behind me. "She just...I don't know how. I saw her. She wasn't there and now she is."

"Listen," I say to the woman. "I don't know if you've been staying here or what, but we just rented the place for a few days. We can leave. You can stay here for the next three days and no one else will be here to bother you."

Am I bitching out and offering my room to a weird girl who eats muffins like they're going out of style? Yes. Yes I am. I just need to get out of here and to somewhere safer. I don't know what this person is capable of, but she seems way too comfortable trespassing.

"Define staying here." She licks her fingertips and wipes the crumbs from her tank top. "Well, you did let me in." She walks over to Maven's bed, her heels clicking with every step, and falls back onto the mattress with her arms stretched out. "Ah. It's been so long. I'm starving."

"Am I in an alternate reality?" I ask Maven.

"We both may be," Maven returns.

I turn my attention to the woman. "Sasha, is it? I didn't let you in, but if someone did they were mistaken. Listen, we're just gonna go." Grabbing my most valuable items, I start shoving my things into the nearest bag. "I don't even need to contact the host, the place is all yours."

I tap Maven's leg with mine and mouth to her, "pack!"

Sasha sits upright on the bed with no help from her arms, just strange, uncanny core strength. It reminds me of Dracula rising from his coffin. Something about her is off, like she's on drugs or she's just not right in the head.

She tilts her head. "You did let me in. You gave me the key, silly." She says it like I should know.

I speedily yank my zipper closed. "I didn't, but it's okay. Really." I look up from my bag to see she's not on the bed anymore. "Where did she go?" I ask Maven, who's still sitting on my bed. All of her stuff is on the other side of the room, which Sasha claimed, so I can't exactly blame her for not moving.

"Here." I see a hand in my peripheral vision, offering my toiletry bag from the bathroom. I turn around and my stomach plummets when I register it's Sasha reaching from behind.

I gasp. "How did you do that?"

"Since you're packing." She has a wide smile that bares too many teeth and cracks her lip.

Now that she's closer to me, I see her in more detail. An unnatural shade of yellow swirls in her eyes, her lips are dry and chapped, a fresh fissure lined with red. And a silver necklace with a pentagram pendant hangs between her breasts.

"And just to be clear, the board was the door," she says. "You left the key on the door step, so I came in."

She bares that Cheshire Cat smile again, as a small bit of dark blood dribbles. I audibly grimace, taking the bag from her extended hand, out of instinct.

"I told you! She did it again—she was there and now she's there!" Maven shouts, pointing.

"Are you being serious?" I ask Sasha. "About the board? How did you do that?"

"As serious as the black plague. Mmm, that was tasty." She fits her finger nail between her teeth as if she's revisiting a delicious memory. "Oh and you can leave, but I'll just follow."

I take a seat next to Maven. Packing takes a pause while I consider whether we're being Punk'd, except that can't be a thing because we're not famous and Ashton Kutcher seems past that.

"The real question you should be asking is *why*, not *how*," Sasha suggests.

Maven grabs a pillow, guarding herself with it like it will do something. I don't feel like she wants to hurt us, but it's clear a pillow won't deter her. "Are you a spirit? A demon?" she asks.

I look at her like she grew horns. "Mave, what the fuck?"

"Did you not see her teleport across the room? We played with a spirit board last night. *It said Sasha.*"

She's not wrong, but this isn't a real thing that happens. We didn't summon a demon or ghost named Sasha.

"How did you know?" Sasha asks Maven, wrinkling her nose.

"I'm fucking losing it. No. We're sharing some type of hysteria," I say holding Maven's hands, and ignoring the thing behind me. "This is not happening, Mave. She's not real."

"Oh it's *so happening*," Sasha says. She has my makeup bag now and is rifling through it like a toddler getting the chance to play with her Mom's makeup. She pulls out the highlighter. "Mind if I try some of this?"

I snatch it back. "Yes. I mind!" Though, she could use some lip balm.

"I don't feel good," Maven says, rubbing her chest.

"Well if you're not leaving, then we're going. Maven come on, we're at least going to get breakfast." I address the thing—the woman, the figment of our imagination—now. "And If you're not gone when we come back then I'm calling the cops, for real this time."

"I wouldn't do that," Sasha echoes. "Unless you want a one way ticket to the psych ward. Surprise! No one can see me except you two lovely gals I've seemed to stumble upon."

"Then come with us," Maven suggests. "Prove it."

"Just one second," I say to the thing. I grab Maven and pull her to the other side of the room. "We're not bringing her with us," I whisper, harshly. "She's—There's something wrong with her. If she's real."

"I can hear you," Sasha announces, still digging through my belongings.

"Blair, it sounds crazy I know, but I know what I saw. She materialized. She's not human." Maven presses both palms to her head, pressing her back against the wall. "I can't believe I'm saying this."

"Looks like we might already have a ticket to the psych ward," Sasha chimes in. "Pull it together ladies! You're here for a trip after all aren't you? What's one more? Let's make it one hell of a girl's trip." She shimmies her shoulders in an off-putting way. Everything she does is off-putting.

Maven starts breathing heavily. "You're not a girl! You're a thing! I rebuke you in the—"

Sasha appears in front of Maven, putting a slender finger over her lips. "Shhhh! We don't need to do all that."

She kisses her cheek, slowly, savoring the press of her lips to Maven's skin. A slight chill runs through me. I blink my eyes, trying to blink the image away. When I open them she's gone from where she stood. I swivel my head. Sasha sits at the vanity now, playing with her long black hair in the mirror. I just saw her defy all laws of human nature. I back up a few steps. Goose bumps cover my arms and now I'm the one speechless. I saw her materialize—just as Maven said. Sasha was there and now she's in another place, no denying it.

"Okay," I breathe out. I don't know where I'm getting my confidence, but it's here so I'm using it. "You said we should be asking *why* you're here, so why? What do you want?"

"I did say that. Hmm, what do I want?" She spins around in the rolling chair, playing with her necklace. "I'm hungry—starving, actually."

"You want food?" Maven asks, confused.

"Yeah. That's not too much to ask for, right?" Sasha playfully twirls a strand of her loose black tendril.

"Why can't you just get it yourself?" I ask.

She rises up from the chair and approaches, until she's standing a few inches above me. "It doesn't work that way. I feed on something different." Then she takes an inhale like she's...sniffing me. "It tastes better when you do it anyway."

I shiver, flushed with a mix of fear and disbelief. Maven and I look at each other, confirming we're both here and processing what she's saying. Then I swallow the lump in my throat. "You feed on what exactly?"

Sasha sighs with annoyance, like she's explaining algebra to a child. "Misery, okay?"

"Misery?" I question.

"You heard it right the first time." She crosses her sickly pale arms over her chest. "Enough skirting around it. Here's the deal." She intently delivers the fine print to Maven and I. "Three sacrifices in three days. That's all I ask." She innocently picks at her black nails. "I can't force you, but if you don't fulfill the request, I can make very bad things happen. And if I were you, I would take my word for it." She winks, but it's a little too forced, a caricature of a person.

I try to read Maven's face as she inches closer to me. Is there a word that surpasses bewilderment? An out-of-body experience?

"What do you mean, exactly, by sacrifice?" Maven prods.

"Whatever you think it means. Let's go get breakfast, yeah?" Sasha wraps her arms around both our shoulders like we're old pals.

If I'm going crazy, my delusion is shared. If this is real, then, fuck, we just summoned a demon named Sasha. And she's not leaving us anytime soon.

Chapter 4

Tasty

We leave on foot. Maven and I don't say a thing for a while, just exchange glances as we make our way down the sidewalk while Sasha skips behind us. I stopped looking back two blocks ago, but I can feel her presence. It's heavy—the best way to explain it—like a weighted blanket is on top of me, but weighing down on all the wrong areas, resulting in unease instead of regulation.

"Is this real?" Maven asks on an exhale.

"Yeah. As real as the black plague, apparently."

"Do you really think other people can't see her?"

"I guess we're about to find out." We enter a small, charming cafe. It's the first one we see. It's painted blue and white and, most importantly, is full of other people.

"I think I lost my appetite," Maven says.

"Me too, but we have to eat something. And we need to see if..." I can't bring myself to finish that statement.

A woman at the counter greets us. "Hi there! How many today, just two?"

Sasha reaches past me for a small display of jams and honey. She opens a jar of the honey and starts eating it, spooning it out with her fingers. She dips her finger into her mouth while she moans with delight, before giving up and tilting her head back to pour it straight into her mouth. I expect her to stop after a moment, but she doesn't. She pours a steady yellow stream, until the jar is empty.

I turn my attention back to the hostess. "Yes. Two."

The hostess directs us to a nearby table and I pick up the menu, looking at it, but not really reading it.

"How can you order food right now?" Maven asks under her breath.

"Should we starve instead?"

I look up and past Maven to see Sasha sitting on the counter, licking the remnants from the jar. Maven turns to witness the same thing I am. People walk in and the hostess directs them to a table, totally oblivious to Sasha sitting on the counter between them.

"I don't think they can see her," Maven says.

"Yeah. I think you're right."

A server comes to our table to take our order. I don't hesitate. "Two mimosas and two tarts, please."

"Mimosas?" Maven questions.

"I don't know about you, but I could really use a drink." She contemplates then nods in agreement.

The server scribbles on her note pad. I hold my hand up. "Wait. Make one vegan."

Maven rests her elbows on the table, raking her hands through her mane. "Thanks. I can't even think right now."

Sasha comes and sits next to us. "This place is cute, tasty even. You know, looks are deceiving." She motions to the room with her hands. "The people here are miserable." She points to a couple near the window. "He has halitosis and it's a dealbreaker, but she doesn't want to be that shallow, so she won't break up with him. Instead, she gags when they kiss." She searches, pointing to a woman on the other side of the cafe. "That woman is getting harassed at work and no one is taking it seriously." Her brow jumps. "Well, they will soon." She looks ahead at the receptionist, mouth parting. "Oh and this one's juicy. Her family died in a car crash a couple years ago...she was the sole survivor. And now she's putting herself through college, forced to work at the same time, while barely staying afloat." Sasha rests her chin on her hands. "She's thinking of ending it."

I can't operate in public with her taunting and trailing after us. "Can you fuck off?" I say, my voice louder than I expected.

"Blair," Maven whispers. "People are looking."

I smile and laugh, trying to play it off. "Sorry." That elicits a small chuckle from the thing that calls herself Sasha.

Sasha curls her chapped lip. "Sure. I can fuck off." And in a blink she's no longer there.

We both look around to make sure she's really gone. "Where'd she go?" Maven asks.

"I don't know," I say. "But anywhere other than here is an improvement."

My shoulders fall, not realizing I was holding them so tightly before. The server brings our mimosas. I take a deep inhale and lift my glass. "Cheers." We both chug the cocktail, gulp after gulp, not taking a breath. "Want another?" I finally ask.

Maven nods. "Make it two more."

We waste time ordering drinks and downing them just as quickly, earning side-eyes from everyone here after a while. "I think we're outstaying our welcome." I giggle.

Two prudish women probably in their sixties make some comment to one another, sharing glances our way. It's probably snarky. "Do you think they ever got tipsy at a cafe before ten in the morning?" Maven questions.

"Doubt it. We're just sophisticated that way. Not everyone can be this high class." I hiccup.

Someone brings us our check. I guess we're getting cut off, so I go to the front desk and hand over my card.

"I have to pee," Maven announces.

"Me too."

We stumble to the bathroom. It's small and has one toilet, but we squeeze in. Maven goes first while I wait with my back turned. Then she starts laughing. "What's so funny?" I ask over my shoulder

"Could you have ever imagined," her speech lags, "this is how our trip would go?"

"No." That's an understatement, but the singular word is all my brain can formulate right now, so I'm going with that.

"Yeah. Me either."

She flushes and I trade places. "I'm gonna order us an Uber," I say, while hovering above the toilet seat.

"Where are we going?"

"The cooking class—I didn't forget."

"What about Sasha? I think that kind of disrupts our plans."

"I'm not letting her disrupt our plans. I'm still doing exactly what I came here to do and so are you," I tell her

We're in no condition to walk back to the house and drive, so we stand outside on uneven ground while we wait for our rideshare driver. I want to stay as far away from that house as we can for the day, in hopes we can better avoid *her*. I don't know where she is and apparently she doesn't follow the rules of human logic or physics, so there may not be any escaping her, but I can sure try. The drinks sure helped to wipe her from my mind.

When the black sedan I ordered pulls up, the driver rolls down his window to greet us. "How are you ladies this morning?" He has a New Orleans drawl.

"That's a loaded question," I mumble, looking at Maven. "Are you Jaylen?"

"Sure am. Are you headed to the Marleaux Mansion?"

"We are," I tell him as we climb into the sedan.

He seems friendly, but I don't think either of us are in a chatty mood. I'm still trying to wrap my head around what's reality and what's fiction at the moment. Where we're going is less than twenty minutes away, but it stretches longer, my thoughts filling every second, creating a thick sludge of time.

Maven nudges me. "What do you think will happen if we don't do what she asks?"

That's a thought that has lingered in a dark corner, one I haven't wanted to acknowledge. "I don't know."

"Maybe she's just trying to scare us into making a deal," she whispers. "That's how it works, right? You have to agree to it, make a deal?"

I've only ever seen movies with this stuff. I don't know how this works in real life. Do you have to choose the demon or does the demon choose you?

"My guess is as good as yours," I tell her. "It could be worth a shot to just ignore it? Maybe she'll go away and move on to someone else."

Maven leans back in her seat. "Maybe."

I look out the window as we slow to pass through the historic neighborhood. People are walking down the street, and I swear I'm seeing a version of Sasha on every block. I keep seeing her in strangers, women with long black hair and black clothes, only to blink and realize my mistake. She's haunting me at this point.

Maven's sudden panic interrupts my own inner paranoia. "Do you think we'll ever get rid of her, that she'll actually go away? If she's a demon and not a figment of our imagination, she could haunt us forever."

"Can you pull over at this gas station coming up?" I ask Jaylen. "I need to get some...gum." I really just need a distraction from this conversation which is completely killing my buzz.

I put a hand on her leg. "Mave, let's just try to get through the day, okay? I can't sit here and go through anymore what-ifs. I'm over here going crazy myself."

"Sure thing," Jaylen answers. "Your stop is just up the road from here."

She scoffs. "So, what then, business as usual?"

I get out of the car and walk into the rundown gas station, where someone is camping out next to the door, half asleep. I scan through all my gum flavor options. I grab a minty one and decide I could actually use a pack of cigarettes too, though I'm not sure when I'll be able to smoke it—not in his car and not during the cooking class.

"Can I get a pack of Marlboro Gold, please?" I ask the cashier whose back is to me, organizing the cartons.

"Careful, they cause cancer." The attendant turns, revealing wild, amber eyes. Sasha's grin grows wider, and I take a step back. *She's everywhere.*

She points to the blue trucker hat resting on top of her long, stringy black hair with the company logo on it. "Like my hat?" She's not in her earlier attire but taking on that of the person who should be standing behind the counter. Putting a finger to her lip, she says, "On second thought..." She pushes two packs toward me with uncanny eye contact. "Have two."

I press my eyes shut and put my fingers to my temples. "What's happening?"

"I said buy two and get one free."

I open my eyes to see someone else's face—a young, freckled-faced woman with full cheeks and kind eyes. "Sorry," I say, slamming five dollars on the counter. I rush away, taking my gum with me.

"You don't want your change?" She calls after me, but I breeze out the door like a bat out of hell.

Not only can she be anywhere, but she can be anyone.

Our driver pulls to the curb. "Here we are, ladies. And if y'all need me to drive y'all again, here's my personal number. I make more when I book rides outside the app. And if you need to de-stress, hit me up."

I'm sure he heard parts of our conversation. It's either that or he can just sense the panic seeping through our pores.

"Thanks, Jaylen," Maven replies, as we step onto the lawn of the slender three-story mansion.

I look up at the splendor and beauty of it. The rectangular lot was likely specifically carved for this once grand home. Now the three-story mansion serves as a bed and breakfast that does part-time event hosting. The gray exterior is trimmed in immaculate detail, with arches over the windows and a wrought iron railing encasing the second-story balcony.

The lower-level windows are sealed with dark shutters, but a large stoop and front door welcome us. Located in the *Faubourg Marigny*, the home is juxtaposed; sitting behind a marker titled *Solomon Northup, twelve years a slave.*

It rests at the former site of a notorious slave pen where a free man of color was once sold into slavery.

"Jesus," I say as we read the historical marker in the grassy median we're standing on.

Part of me wonders if Sasha would have been here for that—it had to have been misery incarnate.

I feel an arm flung over my shoulder. I swivel my head to see Sasha standing between us. "*Now that was tasty*. Speaking of tasty, lead the way, girls."

A cold shiver consumes me whole. Looks can be deceiving. She's occasionally creepy, but more than that, she's a real-life demon who feeds on misery of the worst kind and we fucking summoned her. So now what?

Chapter 5

Hungry and Bored

Contrary to the alternative, which would be spiraling, we do as any sane person would and go about our day. In the great room, cooking stations are set up with the chef based in the center. Various ingredients are organized on each table with perfect portions in metal bowls for each student. It already smells delicious here, scents ranging between buttery and savory.

"Welcome! Please, pick a station," the chef announces. She's a short but strongly built woman, wearing an all-white chef's uniform and even a small chef's hat to match.

Maven and I choose stations next to each other, naturally, while the rest of the attendees pick their respective places. Her and I share a knowing look of *I hope this goes okay.*

Ignoring is the best plan we have. Sasha will get the picture and go away after a while, once she realizes there's no way we're heeding to her whims. No one else can see her, so what damage could she really do besides haunting the ever loving shit out of us?

"All right. Has anyone made shrimp étouffée before?" the chef asks. A few people raise their hands eagerly. "You ain't ever made shrimp étouffée like this, baby."

The dish does sound exquisite, but after the mimosas we just downed, I don't think I have much more room left. And shit, Maven's vegan. *Is it still a vegan meal if I take the shrimp out?* She's a better friend than I am because she hasn't said or asked anything about what we're making. Unless, there are more important things on her mind which is probably the case.

The sound of Sasha's boots hitting the polished wood floor makes its way around the room. She sniffs the air as she passes each table, then stops where a bald man with thick-rimmed glasses is stationed at. She proceeds to dip her long finger that grazed Maven's lip earlier into a small measuring bowl containing some type of spice. He looks right through her. Ah, to be so lucky.

"First things first, we're gonna start with the roux. Grab your flour and butter," the chef instructs. She lifts a glass jar containing a pre-made version of the roux—a dark brown liquid. "It should look like this when it's ready. It takes time, but the darker the better."

I combine my butter and flour in the skillet, stirring it with a wooden spoon and watching it create a creamy emulsion.

"Don't let it sit or it will burn. Keep stirring. While we're stirring, I'll tell you a little about the origin of the dish."

Sasha leans over my station. "Making enough for two?"

"Go away," I seethe.

"What was that?" the chef asks in my direction.

"Oh nothing, sorry. A fly."

"Nice save." Sasha sticks her finger in my roux, drawing a heart into the base of the skillet, while maintaining eye contact and flashing a devilish smile. I wince in disgust.

Maven's eyes dance between her station and mine. "Ignore her," I whisper.

Sasha takes that as an opportunity to slink over to Maven's station. She picks up a metal bowl of chopped celery, raises it in the air, then turns it over, dropping it to the ground. "Oops. Try ignoring me now, Blondie."

Everyone turns to see the source of the clatter. Chopped celery is scattered across the floor as the bowl spins around in small rotations. "I'm so sorry," Maven says. "I'm so clumsy sometimes."

"That's okay. We have extra," the chef responds. Her assistant quickly arrives with a new bowl of celery, then leaves to go fetch a broom and dustpan.

I return my focus to the roux, but someone—or something—is hovering over me once again. "It's a nice plan you have, but not the right one," Sasha says.

In my peripheral, she picks a raw shrimp from the bowl of ice water waiting next to my burner, and slowly brings it to her mouth. She leans in closer so I can hear the chewing of soft, raw meat. It squelches with a wetness that sends a tingle down my spine.

"When I find something I want, I stay the course," she whispers. Then, picking the shrimp's tail from her teeth, she tosses it into my skillet.

My response is no response. I just keep stirring.

The chef claps. "All right, the roux should be going strong. Now, we're gonna work on the holy trinity."

"Oh no!" Sasha shouts, clutching her chest emphatically, followed by a laugh.

"Grab your celery, onion, and green bell pepper, then combine it with a little butter until the onion's translucent," the chef echoes.

Sasha sighs. "I'm getting bored now, hungry *and* bored."

I grit my teeth together as she starts to pick away at more of my shrimp. Her chewing—wet and slushy—is threatening to send me over the edge. My brain is begging me to do anything to make it stop—to make her stop chewing in my godforsaken ear. I never knew I had misophonia, but at this moment, I'm convinced I do.

I'm struggling to focus on sauteing the vegetables, when I start to smell something overcooked. I look around thinking it must be coming from somewhere other than what's in front of me. Smoke rises. Everything in my pan is burnt. I turned the heat up too high or was so distracted by what Sasha's been doing that I let my roux burn. Now my own boiling point is nearing completion.

How long does a haunting take to make someone go clinically insane? I wonder. I'm sure she knows. I'm sure she's had plenty of practice in the matter. God. I can't deal with this.

Chew.

How could I possibly get rid of her?

Chew.

Can she just stop already!

Chew.

The sound is tickling a part of my brain that is supposed to go untouched. I slap her hand away when she reaches for my last shrimp. "Stop eating my fucking shrimp!" I yell. It's not like it will make a difference. What can I make with a burnt roux and a single shrimp? But I feel better by my outburst for a split second.

I was louder than I intended to be. I glance over to Maven and she's holding her hand over her mouth. A scan of the rest of the room reveals everyone else is looking at me in various states of confusion.

"That went well," I say, sitting on the front door steps of the mansion.

"I can't blame you," Maven says. "She was trying to push your buttons. So much for business as usual."

"I was really looking forward to eating that too," Sasha adds.

Maven fixes her gaze on Sasha. "You're not going to leave us alone are you?"

"No. I told your friend I get what I want, even if it takes years. And I have the time." She picks at her long black acrylics—I think they're acrylics at least.

Okay—so we can't ignore her. Well we can, but she makes it *really hard* to. I'm not sure how much more of this I can take. Would buckling this soon, considering going through with her request just so she leaves us alone be weak? I guess a part of me is. I can't continue to deal with this for years. I doubt anyone could.

Sasha stands, twirling her hair. "I told you I can make bad things happen. How about this for some motivation: if you don't deliver the three sacrifices in three days, I take one of your souls." She tilts her head, lowering her gaze. "Like I said, I can't make you do it, but I can make you *wish* you did."

Shit. This is real, there's no escaping it—escaping her. And she's threatening to take our souls? How can she even do that?

She wanders around us, trailing a finger across each of our shoulders as she speaks. "I'll drive you so mad until you take your *own* life." Her unsettling Cheshire Cat grin returns, showing a wide display of teeth.

"And then you'll spend the rest of eternity with me and we can braid each other's hair!"

Ugh. I get up, pulling Maven along with me. Yet again, Sasha follows behind at a surprisingly comfortable distance. "We're going for a walk," I announce, my blood pressure rising every minute she's near.

I grip Maven's hand in mine as we mindlessly walk through the empty French Quarter streets, a sort of comfort to the uncomfortable thoughts sailing around. *What does sacrifice mean?* She wasn't totally forthcoming on the severity. There's no way on earth we can give her that, however, she's proven she means business.

We pass old buildings with chipped brick and aged wood, ferns pouring out from balconies like they were born there. Luckily few people are out.

"Blair." Maven breaks the silence between us. "What are we gonna do?"

I march forward, my thoughts a blur. I can't discern right from left or good from bad, I just know I can't live like this. Despite it all, I decide what we need to do next. "What she asks us to do."

"We can't do that." Maven stops, anchoring me as I try to continue on the uneven sidewalk. "I would rather die myself than kill someone."

I release my grip from hers and turn around. "Maybe we won't have to. She didn't say it had to be human."

A disgusted expression tugs on Maven's mouth. "I guess it is better than the alternative."

I don't like the idea either. I don't like any of this, but as much as I hate it, I want Sasha gone more.

Chapter 6

Unpack It

The cobble stoned streets are mostly empty. It's too early in the day for a crowd the neighborhood usually attracts. I look back to see it's empty behind us too.

"She's gone," I tell Maven.

"For now. Where do we even find an animal to..." Maven cocoons herself by wrapping her arms around her torso.

"Let's worry about that later. We can go to a pet store or something. Frankly, I don't want to think about it right now. If I don't have a semblance of normalcy today, I may just beat her to it and bury myself."

"Don't say that," Maven demands. "And you can't just push away things that are uncomfortable Blair."

My upper lip curls with annoyance. "Is that supposed to have a deeper meaning? We're in a pretty unique circumstance. Sue me for not wanting to deal with a bitch demon."

"Maybe it does have a deeper meaning," she retorts. "But that's why I'm saying it. Because we're here and I'm not letting my fate rest in the hands of someone who refuses to acknowledge anything painful."

I stop in my tracks. She's pissed, she's out of her mind, but so am I. "Why are you being like this? It's not you."

"Look around. Maybe it's because our lives are probably about to be ruined, B, *and look at what we've done with them.*" She exhales, releasing pent up anger.

Now is not the time to throw rocks.

I scoff. "You haven't done so bad, but yeah let's focus on me. I'm the one who pushes her problems away, according to you."

"I'm sorry," she mutters.

I raise my hands. "No, no, let's talk about it. Yeah my problems got pushed under the rug. I never got put into therapy, so I did my own therapy by treating men like they're disposable and practicing hyper-independence." I point to my chest. "I run away from what doesn't serve me. At least I know my reason for being the way I am." Rock thrown.

"Hah. That's rich," she says, shaking her head.

Of all the times to get down to the marrow of our issues, she chooses now?

"That's all you have to say?" I ask. "You say I push away what's uncomfortable. Let's unpack that, we're already here."

We're standing in front of some tourist shop with an open door. An employee steps out. "Interested in a psychic reading?"

I glare her way. "We're busy!" The employee goes back inside without a word.

Maven crosses her arms over her chest. "You want to know my reason for being where I am now? I don't even know, Blair. I wish I could answer that." She sniffs as her nose grows red and I feel like an asshole because my rock hit her square. She doesn't deserve the vitriol I'm spewing just because she called me out. I don't know what else to do, so I wait.

"I told you in confidence I wasn't happy," she says in an un-even tone. "How dare you use it against me? Even if I don't want it, I'm stuck. Being with Matt is comfortable. It's all I know, I've been with him since I was *sixteen*." Tears begin to build. "My other friends talk about how their husbands dote after them and do things to show them how much they care. Meanwhile, Mathew doesn't care enough to water the freaking plants." Her face scrunches beneath the pressure and I grab for her hand because I'm not against her. I could never be.

"What have we been doing, Mave?"

She shrugs. "What we had to do, to survive."

I embrace her in a tight hug that I don't ever want to end. We both need it. I need something stronger than a hug, actually, but this will do for now.

I bury my face in her hair that smells like peaches. "You know what? She's doing this to us, digging up what we want to bury." I space her away from me, my hands on her shoulders while I acknowledge her directly. "We're gonna have fun despite Sasha. Isn't that perfumery you wanted to go somewhere around here?"

"I appreciate your enthusiasm, but I don't know how to go on with my day while knowing what she wants us to do, along with the threat of what happens if we don't."

"Didn't you just say all we've been doing is wasting time?" I inter-twine her arm with mine. "We're not gonna let anyone or *anything* determine how we spend it from here on out."

I almost believe myself.

The smell hits me before we step through the door. It's as if the best pages of a luxury magazine hit you in the face. A large chandelier centers the small boutique with glass shelves and mirrored walls. We're the only ones in here, luckily. Not many people could fit in here truth be told, but I'm also thankful for the lack of because I'm not fit to be around the public based on my recent outburst.

A petite woman with a messy bun and silk headband greets us. "Welcome! Let me know if I can help you with anything. We carry exclusively perfumes imported from Paris and offer discovery sets if you can't decide on a specific scent."

"Thank you. We'll be sure to let you know," Maven responds with reddened eyes.

I scan the shelves with various luxury perfume brands, spritzing them on the little paper strips provided. They all smell great, mostly. More than smelling good, it's a decent distraction. Distract one sense with another.

"Smell this one," Maven suggests.

Her eyes are getting brighter. I think this was a good decision. We just have to go on, it's go on or crumble under the pressure and neither one of us are up for anymore crumbling today if we have any say in it.

She sprays her chosen perfume on a strip. It could easily be one of the best ones I've smelled. It has hints of vanilla, musk, tamarind, and citrus. It's a perfect blend of feminine and masculine.

"It's a long-lasting perfume," the boutique owner tells us. "Every time I wear it I get compliments. It's a best seller."

It has a price tag to match, but worth every penny. "We'll take two," I say.

We smell a few more before making a full decision, taking a whiff of the coffee beans in between each inhale for a cleanse. While chatting with the owner between sniffs, she tells us about the history of the building, and offers a small tour of the connected apartment in the back. There's a copper-topped bar that keeps glasses cold. And apparently celebrities would sneak from the old hotel next door, in order to escape from all the prying eyes. I'm not much of a history buff, but anything to take my mind elsewhere. I only wished there was a door I could sneak out of and into a hidden apartment to avoid the inevitable.

"Thanks for the tour," I tell her at check out, where the owner hands me a small black bag in exchange. "That's okay, I can just throw it in my purse."

She hands me the perfume box and I turn to see Maven standing still, facing away from the counter. "Hey. Are you ready to head out?" I ask. She doesn't respond, so I walk around to face her.

She's in a trance-like state, but snaps out of it when we come face to face. "I thought I saw her pass by the window. No. I did see her..." Her face scrunches. "She licked it. She looked at me and licked the glass."

"Maybe you did, but *fuck her*, remember? Today is for us." I swallow around the lump in my throat, knowing Sasha is relentless in her hunger.

Chapter 7

Sacrifice

We've stayed within the neighborhood's borders, feeling some type of unspoken safety here because so far, it's the longest we've been free of Sasha. We've gone in and out of multiple shops, explored galleries with colorful art, and a boutique with colorful but barely-there clothing. I don't know about Maven, but my feet are tired.

"I need to eat," I announce, as we continue through Jackson Square, finally settling on a park bench.

"Me too. I guess we should grab something," she hesitantly replies.

It's an association now between Sasha and food, especially shrimp. I'm not sure when I'll be able to stomach seafood again.

"Do you think she'll show up?" Maven asks.

My chest tightens. "I don't know, but we can't starve ourselves to avoid her. It's not food she wants anyways. She said she feeds on misery, though she seems to put away anything." A thought comes to my mind. "One thing though. Do you think we should see someone while we're here, like a witch or something? People here live and breathe that kind of stuff. Maybe someone could help us ward her off somehow."

"I think we screwed up by messing with that stuff in the first place," Maven adds. "Messing with it more could only make it worse."

"You don't know that." A couple, hand in hand, walk past us and I wait until they go out of earshot. "If there's a bad part to whatever, the other side, then there has to be a good part, too."

She looks at me for a long while. "I'll think about it."

"Okay." There's a small flutter of hope within me, but at the same time I've accepted our fate in some measure. I know what she wants and I know she's not going to relent until we offer it. *She has the time.* And we don't.

On our way to get food, we pass by a shop filled with curiosities in the window that make my stomach bubble. Taxidermized foxes are in little tuxedos, along with other parts and things that make you double take to decide for certain you see what you think you do. But something in particular catches my eye. There's a book on the other side of the glass, propped up with a cover that reads *The ABC's of Demons.* I've never been more interested in that specific type of literature than I am now.

I rush for the door. "I need to go in here. Just for two minutes."

"What on earth could you need in there?" Maven asks.

I point to the book in the window. "You don't really believe her name is Sasha, do you? Maybe her real one is in there."

"Your mind's a scary place, but you're a genius," she says.

We step into the dark cabinet of curiosities. There are taxidermized animals on too many shelves, specimens in jars suspended in a clear liquid with a yellowish hue, and herbs that hang from the ceiling. Moths are pressed in frames, and there's an unusual usage of animal parts and bones, but what I'm most interested in is a stack of books that can't be found in a library.

I scan the spines, looking for one that matches the black cover in the window with Gothic, silver foiled lettering. Finally landing on *The ABC's of Demons,* I pull it from the shelf and open the hard cover to the last page. *By Demonologist, Robert Evangelicast.* What a name, it sounds like it came straight out of a B-rated movie. This may turn out to be as helpful as a concrete parachute, but there's a chance I'll learn something useful.

We approach one of the places on our itinerary, an eclectic restaurant. Inside, we're met with deep blue velvet chairs and sofas. It's a trendy spot with an artful set up and great food, according to the reviews. There's a neon sign on the hostess podium that says, *Seat yourselves.* We choose a table next to an old brick wall with vibrant art strung up, while mannequin bodices hang adjacent to some tables—some with pasties, others in lingerie.

I may look at food in a different way after watching the one we don't speak of slurping raw crustaceans like there's no tomorrow, but I'm still hungry. I order a grilled chicken salad and a fruity cocktail. As vital as time is, I can't seem to track it right now. Maven and I both are sitting here, lost in our own thoughts or lost in trying to avoid them. I stare at one of the mannequin bodies wondering whose idea it was to use them as decor, but it works.

The server brings our dishes out in what seems as quickly. As I pierce my fork through the small tomato, juice squirts back at me covering my cheek. I imagine if that's what it's like to stab someone. Does it paint you? I physically recoil at the un-welcome, more than intrusive thought.

"What's that look about?" Maven eyes me as she sets down her glass of sweet tea.

"Nothing." I fake a smile. "Just a little mess." I grab a napkin and dab my cheek, wondering if it will come to that in order to get the demon off our heels. I pick through the rest of my salad. "So...did you think about it? Going to see a psychic?"

"Not really," Maven admits, pushing her vegan salad away. "But what do we have to lose?"

"My appetite's kind of slim too," I say, staring at the small tomato leaking orange juice.

"Why don't we take a look at that book first?" she suggests. "It could be helpful."

I pull it out of the white plastic bag and scoot over to Maven's side, opening the book up to the first page.

Warning: A name holds power, not just to summon, which I whole heartedly advise against, but also to banish. May you use the information in this book with pure intentions, for education and above all, respect.

"Promising so far," I note.

We start at *A*, passing through utterly diabolical and difficult-to-pronounce names with brief descriptions of what characteristics each obtains, as well as aliases, signs of presence, etc. There's one in the *C* section who's named Calvagriel.

Aliases: The Skeletal Songweaver or the Harrowed Harbinger.

It could all be made up, likely so. It feels too produced. Apparently, though, this guy manifests as a tall skeletal figure with a cloaked hood covering his face.

Signs of Presence: Cracked mirrors and radio interference.

Origin: He was once an Angel tasked with comforting the dying. When he was stricken from his righteous role—a result of siding with Lucifer—he became what he is now, someone who weaves fear and sorrow into the dying with his undetectable song.

Sounds ridiculous.

Feeding Method: Sharp pain inflicted from his notes, ensuring those on their deathbeds go uneasily and without peace.

I just need to find one whose feeding method is misery so that I may get down to the grit of who she really is. If this book only has a little bit of truth to it, we may find a way to get rid of her.

I reach *D,* purely focusing on *Feeding Methods.* Life source from the sickly. No. Another being grief. No. Next heartbreak. No. Finally, *misery.*

"Dolorath." I gasp. "This could be her." I cut my eyes to Maven.

"How reliable do you think this Robert Evangelicast is?" Maven asks.

"I don't know. But like you said, what do we have to lose?"

I read up on Dolorath out loud to Maven, a fictional or actual demon who we may know as Sasha. "She tends to manifest as a beautiful woman." I look to Maven with promise.

"Debatable," she says.

"She was once known as a karmic angel, serving as one who would create balance among men. She could be generous, gracious, and at times would avenge God's fury at man's failure, but upon many angel's fall from grace, she became Misery's Maw, feasting on the misery she inflicts."

My chest has a caving feeling, anxiety rumbling at the possibility of us getting closer to understanding her game and possibly how to beat her at it. Though I'm unsure how that will play out.

I continue reading. *"Signs of Presence: Insect infestations, sulfuric odor, shadows."* Seems familiar. Could this all be a coincidence or is it more than that?

I move onto the next line. *"Aliases: Misery Business, Misery's Maw, and... Hot Shit.* What?"

Slamming the book shut, I drop my head in my hands. "Okay this is bullshit. It's a fucking joke! It was ridiculous to even think I could best her."

"Hey. You tried," Maven says. "Don't feel bad. We have a backup plan, remember? Let's go find someone who can help."

Leaving the restaurant, we search for a reputable psychic. The first two shops we passed were nothing but tourist traps from the looks of it— tees that say *New Orleans*, altar candles with celebrities on them fashioned as Virgin Mary, and some person at the doorway advertising their readings.

The third time is the charm. Finally, arriving at a small mystic shop with no gimmicks visible from the outside, we enter to see spiritual items lining the walls: little voodoo dolls, crystals, candles, card decks, and incense among other things that scream they at least believe in what they're doing—no shot glasses with the Bourbon street sign or Jackson Square etched onto them.

Burning incense fills the air and my lungs, producing a few coughs from both of us in quick succession. The ventilation system must be sluggish because the air is thick with the odor.

A woman with dark skin and tight curls walks up from the back rooms to greet us. At least, I think she's here to greet us. She looks us up and down, like she's surveying if we're worth her time or not. The air permeates between us with a tone of unease before she speaks.

"What are you here for?" the woman asks.

"We were hoping for some... guidance," I tell her. "My name is Blair and this is—"

"I don't need to know your names. I'm not sure I can help you." She goes over to the door and flips the sign to closed.

"Not sure if you can help us?" I repeat.

Maven steps forward. "We need your help more than you know." Maven pleads to the woman, the very same person who was so unsure about coming here earlier. She looks desperate in her plea. It's the reality of our situation, though. We're here because that's just what we are, desperate.

The woman's face stays stoic, but she lifts her chin. "Madam Clemence Delacroix."

"Maven," she announces herself, even though names weren't up for discussion a second ago.

I'm not sure how her plea changed things, but whatever works. Because the honest truth is: if Madame Clemence Delacroix can't offer a solution, we're just as fucked as we were before coming here.

"Follow me," Madam Clemence says.

We're both a little apprehensive, but I lead the way following her past the front desk and through a beaded doorway, leading to a dark hallway. The beaded strings drag across my shoulders as Madame Clemence gestures to a door-frame emitting a dim glow.

Inside the room, there's a better smell than the one in the front of the shop, making it easier to breathe. This room smells minty and clean. It clears my lungs and sends a sense of calm over me. There's a small table scattered with an array of essential oils, crystals, and a metal bowl with wood burning inside of it. There's a chair for Madame Clemence on one side of the table and two chairs for us on the opposite.

"You need my help or you need guidance?" she asks, lifting the short wooden stick from the bowl and waving it in front of our faces.

"Both?" I say. "We—saw something." I look over to Maven and she nods in Madam Clemence's direction. "And we want to know if you can help us to get rid of it."

"You both saw this unnatural thing at the same time?"

"Yes," I admit.

She gathers her crystals, arranging them on the table. "That's not good." That response sends shivers down my spine. I don't know this woman, but if she has a whole career dedicated to the supernatural she must know more than I do.

Maven fidgets, twisting her ring in circles around her finger. "Why is that not good?"

"If an entity can present itself to more than one person's consciousness, simultaneously," she clasps her hands together, "that means it beholds extreme power." Quickly, she moves to the side of the room, pulling something from the drawer of a cabinet that has animal bones displayed on top of it. Coming back, she extends her hand out to us and in an upturned palm, reveals two rings—black rocks centered in copper wiring.

"What's this?" I ask.

"Black Tourmaline. It protects against demonic entities and evil doings."

I huff. "What makes you think it's demonic?" I know what Sasha is. I just don't want to accept or say it out loud. Either way, I accept the ring.

"Because you have a demonic attachment—each of you." She glances between us. "That's why you could barely breathe when you walked in. My incense offends evil."

"I certainly do not," Maven declares. "She is *not* attached to us. We haven't given her permission. Isn't that how it works, we have to give her permission?"

"Keep the tourmaline with you at all times. You can give it an electric charge by rubbing it. It should ward her off for a little while," Madam Clemence says. "It appears to you as a female?"

"Yes. She said to call her Sasha," Maven answers.

Madam Clemence shakes her head. "That's not its real name and that's not its true form. *Don't be deceived*."

Maven slips on her ring and raises her hands, palms out. "Oh we're not deceived. We want her gone."

Madame Clemence sits back in her seat. "When did you first cross paths with this Sasha?"

"Well her name could be Dolorath, according to a joke of a book from that curiosity shop down the street." I bite the inside of my cheek, embarrassed to admit how we came into her path of destruction. "The truth is, we played with a Ouija board. It was in the attic of our rental."

She looks as if I just told her I killed a puppy, which shit, I really hope I don't have to. She stands, sending her chair skirting across the wood with a squeal. "You need to leave."

"What?" Maven asks, exasperated. "I thought you were going to help us?"

"No one can help you besides yourselves. Take the tourmaline and go on your way." Madam Clemence hurriedly ushers us to the door and locks it behind us.

"What the hell?" I breathe out. "Is it just me or was it weird that when I mentioned the Ouija board she got all sketchy?"

"You'd think the demon part would scare her more than a Ouija board. She knows something," Maven says through narrowed eyes.

I focus on the black rock in my hand. "Doesn't matter. Let's hope these things work." I stuff it in my purse. I may just stock up on an entire collection of black rocks if that's what it takes to keep Sasha away.

With regret, we arrive back to the Airbnb at nightfall.

"Remind me why we're here?" Maven asks, trailing out the question.

"Because this is where our stuff is. Coming back to the scene of the crime doesn't exactly increase our chances of running into her anymore than it does at a hotel."

I'm really hoping these rocks show up for us, but Sasha has proven so far that she can show up anywhere.

"I guess you're right." She fiddles with her new ring, twisting it.

I step through the unlocked front door and quickly flick the lights on. "Clear so far."

Maven walks in behind me and we scan the house, making our way through to the bedroom. I plop onto the bed after a long day of trying to avoid the house and kick my shoes off. I turn my head to see Maven doing the same thing. "First day down, huh?"

"Don't make jokes." She stares at the ceiling, processing whatever the hell today was. I can't help but do the same.

All that occupies the room is the sound of passing cars, their occasional beeps and seconds of music blaring. I focus on the white blank space of the ceiling, melting into the mattress, hoping it's what consumes me. My eyelids become heavy but the weight is just as quickly lifted by a faint buzzing.

It swishes past my ear again and again while I lay still, allowing my eyes to search for the source. Reliant, it's the same fly from this morning resting on the ceiling fan blade. I know because it's a fat one—a fat black speck. If we trap it in here, robbing it of the sustenance it requires, how long until it dies? Or will it slip through the cracks, finding a way to get what it needs in order to survive?

It sits on the fan blade for a while, until he buzzes off in the direction of the bathroom. Minutes pass and I've contemplated the life of a fly for long enough. "I need a shower," I finally admit, forcing myself to move.

Maven groans. "Me too, but I don't want to get out of bed."

Somehow the idea of moving puts our peace at risk. I feel like we're skating on thin ice, as if she's just around the corner and if we take a misstep we'll crash through and into icy waters where she'll be there in the depths, a siren waiting to drag us to our deaths.

Reluctantly, I rise up. "We're acting as if things are normal right? When I'm done we can watch a movie. We'll start tomorrow."

Maven tucks herself under the blanket. "No romances. Or horror. But something happy."

"Wouldn't think of it. By the way...do you want to talk about anything?"

We never really processed that bomb she dropped earlier, about her unfulfilled marriage. I'd hate to sweep it under the rug, though if I were in her position, I know that's exactly what I would do.

She shakes her head. "Maybe later."

That's okay with me. I'm not up for processing my relationship trauma right now either. I reach to grab my hastily packed toiletry bag to see it's not where I thought I left it, so instead I just grab some pajamas from my equally messy suitcase. I probably left it in the bathroom this morning when I was in a hurry to get out of here.

"I won't take too long," I tell Maven, over my shoulder.

I flip on the bathroom light. I can't wait to scrub off the day and everything that came with it. Turning to the tub that eagerly awaits me, I let out an ear splitting scream.

Sasha's laying there, wearing nothing but the silver chain dangling on bare skin. She's chest deep in bubbles, looking at me with a fake surprise. She yells out, clutching the bubbles toward her frame. "Ah! I'm indecent." She follows it up with a maniacal laugh.

Maven rushes into the bathroom. Grabbing my arm from behind, she's taken her ring off and is holding it out to ward her off.

"Cute rock," Sasha quips, cupping bubbles in her hand then blowing them at us.

Shit. It doesn't work after all.

Sasha stands, her naked body dripping in suds. One long and pale leg follows the other over the edge of the tub, sloshing a puddle of water onto the tile beneath her. I attempt to look away. I hate to admit it, but she has a body any woman would envy. Except she's not a woman. Her waist is slender, her breasts hang in a perfect balance, and her legs are smooth and cellulite-free. I guess if she can pick any form she wants, why would she not pick this one?

She cocks her hip with an arched brow. "You can stare if you want."

I fidget with the pajamas still in my hands and force a dry swallow down.

Maven places her ring on the sink, grabs a towel hanging on the wall and throws it at her. "Put some clothes on."

Sasha sticks her tongue out at the comment. She dries her long black tendrils, while keeping a distance. "So have you put any more thought to my ultimatum?"

I lift my chin, hoping to appear confident. She never said human, so I'm crossing my fingers and toes there's a loophole. "We have. We'll do what you asked. A sacrifice."

Sasha wraps the towel around her body and tilts her head. "Yes. *Three* sacrifices. And day one is almost over, so now you have two days to deliver all of them. But you know what they say, *"The only way to live is to know that you won't forever."* So use that as motivation to get things moving."

My heart ticks up a pace. This is real. We have to deliver unless we want her to implement the misery she consumes on us, by taking our soul. I still don't know how that's possible, but sensible things went out the window at the start of the day.

"We got the picture," I say, as another rush of confidence overcomes me. Then I decide to test the bullshit meter of Robert Evangelecast, "Dolorath."

She takes a step back in disbelief, but a smile slowly reaches her eyes and she almost looks proud? She chuckles. "I don't go by that anymore."

What the actual fuck? So, the demonologist with a name from a B-rated movie *is not* a crock of shit?

Maven starts laughing. She's actually losing it, I'm worried about her. In between breaths, "You actually. Go by the name. Hot Shit?"

"I go by many names," Sasha spews. "That's just one of them." She crosses her arms over her chest. "Regardless, congratulations. What exactly do you two think you've accomplished?"

My spine stands a little straighter. "A name has power."

"Cute. Do you see anything happening?" She holds out her arms. "Say it again. I dare you."

"Dolorath." She stares me down, unaffected. I say it louder with more intention this time. "Dolorath!"

She turns her head to the side and stifles a laugh. "Sorry. I really am." She looks at us like helpless little puppies with no defense. "A name is a name, nothing more."

My strong spine collapses, each vertebra folding into one another and I shrink.

"Well now that's established, the bathroom's all yours." Sasha smiles. "Mind letting me through?" We back up to the sink to give her room to walk past, though she doesn't need it. There's plenty of space in the bathroom. She glares at us with daggers for eyes. "Can a girl get some privacy?"

I squint, then laugh almost as maniacally as she did minutes ago. "You can't get close to us. Can you? It fucking works," I tell Maven. Sasha works her jaw. "Mave, rub the rock!"

Maven hastily picks it up from the sink and charges it by rubbing it in her hands like we were instructed. Sasha scowls with a twitch of her eye, her mask slowly slipping. Her eyes, previously an amber shade of yellow, darken to pitch-black. She's starting to look more like the demon she is, with empty hollows that want to devour. She rears her mouth into a snarl and for a moment, I'm fearful of what she may do next. The words of Madam Clemence echo in my mind, *"That's not her true form."* I should have paid more attention to the book, to prepare myself for whatever disgusting form is about to reveal itself.

Sasha takes one step forward, but halts in her steps. She lets out a low growl that sounds like it could only come from an inhumane thing, something that you only want to hear, though you don't want to hear it at all. Hearing it is better than seeing it because conjuring the true image of whatever that sound erupts from would send you into psychosis. I might be there already. Her angles become sharper while her voice changes into a more menacing one, sending a strange feeling over my body. It's like worms are crawling all over me, inside even. "It won't keep you safe forever. Keep me away, ward me off, I'll just come back when you least expect it," Sasha warns.

Maven puts the ring back onto her finger and just then, Sasha vanishes. Maven begins to hyperventilate. She leans against the counter, sinking to the tile floor, vacantly staring ahead, chest rising and falling quickly.

I catch my breath. "It worked."

The joy fades a moment too soon as my own adrenaline leaves my body and I join Maven on the floor. We both curl our knees into our chests, letting time pass until the image of Sasha's face and sound of her low growl leaves us.

"She's right, B," Maven whispers. We can wear the rings until we forget or until she takes our fingers—I wouldn't put it past her—but it won't keep her away forever. We still have to do it, don't we?" She looks up to me like I'm the leader, like I'm somehow the one that has what it takes to save our skins.

My silence is an indication that we still have to do it, but maybe it won't be so bad.

Chapter 8

Misery

A small green snake, half-hidden in the foliage, coils in the corner. But I can still see its beady black eyes. I wonder if Sasha has a hidden forked tongue, just like the black eyes she shares with the snake.

Glass cage after glass cage, reptiles hunker down, waiting for their next meal. I've heard they lack empathy, maybe that's why the story of Satan begins as a snake. She's cold-blooded the same way, except she gets to play pretend with her skin suit and new name. Part of me is glad I haven't seen the full face that's underneath, her truest form. The teaser from last night was close enough: black eyes, sharp features, an otherworldly tone coming from the depths of her throat. She could be doing us a favor in that aspect or she just likes playing games, either way I'll take what she's given. At least we got a demon that's not horrible to look at, compared to the hooded skeleton that calls himself the Harrowed Harbinger. I'm tempted to go back and flip through the pages now that I know it's not a total crock, but it would only send me deeper into despair.

I twist the new extension of myself in circles around my finger, like I've been doing every hour since I woke up this morning.

"This way," Maven says. I follow her through the isles. "I know my way around the pet store. Junior went through so many fish over the years...and hamsters." She winces as we arrive at the area where the small critters call home.

Small feet scamper through the cardboard nesting while others hide away in their small plastic shelters and away from our eyes. They're anxious little fuzz balls, but they're still kind of cute. They have a reason to be scared, because one of them will be our sacrifice.

Their little tan and white bodies are huddled together, searching for either safety or warmth. "It's hard to choose which one, isn't it?" I admit.

"I'm not picking which one gets a death sentence," Maven says in a low voice. "One of the workers can do that." She looks around and spots a young female attendant with a red collared shirt on and waves her over with a friendly grin. The girl abandons whatever she was about to do to come over. "We would like one of these hamsters, please."

"Have you ever taken care of a hamster?" the girl asks.

Little does she know we have no intention of doing so—to no fault of our own. We just need its soul, I think. *Do hamsters have souls?* I don't know, maybe it's not the soul Sasha wants, just the misery it will feel from the death we deliver. The thought makes me shudder.

"We've had a lot of hamsters over the years," Maven tells her. "N-Not that they all died—I'm not bad at taking care of them. They were for my son. He just got older and you know hamsters, they don't live very long. He's an adult now."

She's nervously rambling, so I cut in to secure the hamster deal. "It's for me. She's helping me get the things I need."

"Okay," says the attendant. She doesn't seem to really care, it's probably more of a routine question they have to ask in order to make sure people know what they're getting into. Even if that life is bite-sized, it's still a life. "I'll be right back," she says.

"This is screwed up," Maven murmurs.

I grab her shoulder, bringing her closer to me. "It's better than the alternative, Mave. We won't go to prison for *this*. We can live with this, okay? We don't have a choice."

"It doesn't feel right. It feels off." She shrugs.

The girl comes back, hauling a small rolling cart in front of her and stopping next to the hamster enclosure. "Which one do you want?" She pulls on a pair of gloves with a snap, maintaining eye contact with me.

"Um. You pick one."

She shoots me a questionable look. "People usually pick their own pet."

I give a disarming smile. *It's not a pet, and I'm not in most people's position.* "Well they all look pretty similar don't they?" I gesture to the cage.

Lifting the top of the enclosure and lowering her hand into it, she cradles one into her palm. The hamster is beige and innocent and tiny. She then grabs a cardboard carton with tiny holes and places the small animal into it before handing it to me. "This is temporary. You can transfer it to a cage with nesting and proper accommodations once you get home."

I give a tight-lipped smile and nod. "We'll be sure to do that, thank you."

"Anything else?"

"No. Just the hamster." The words leave me, then return with a heavy guilt. *Nope just the sacrificial hamster.*

Neither of us have the nerves to drive, so we wait for a rideshare outside. I stand on the curb, the cardboard box hanging in my hand. A small dose of misery rests inside of it—and I'm the Grim Reaper.

The heaviness lingers between us, not only for what awaits, but the ticking time bomb itself. Today is day two of three and we've just started, but neither one of us speaks that knowledge into existence because that makes it too real. If this doesn't work, well—I can't let my mind go to that place just yet.

My phone rings for the first time since I've taken vacation. My company supervisor's name reflects back at me. He knows I'm on leave, but it's a welcome distraction, so I answer it. "Ronald, what can I do for you?"

"Blair. Hi. Sorry to bother you while you're on time off, but I wanted to check in on the London branch transfer and extend the offer to reach out if you need anything. We want to make this a smooth transition for you."

Oh. *My new job.* I can't really be excited about that right now. I'm not even sure I'll make it until then, but he can't know that. "Thank you. Yeah I'll be sure to let you know, but I think I've got it handled so far." I don't. I haven't even begun to make accommodations. That was supposed to be my focus after I got back. "I'll reach out once I'm settled at the new branch," I tell him.

"You're our top worker, Blair, we're happy to have you."

Top worker. If I die, that's one of the things I'll be known for. And it doesn't feel great to know that because there's not much else. What will they put on my headstone? *Daughter, friend, top worker?*

I stuff the phone back in my purse and look up to see Maven glaring at me. "You're really still going?"

"Why wouldn't I?"

"Why would you?" She shakes her head. "Look what's happening Blair. We may not live to see next week."

"I can't rip my career and life apart in the case we don't." I lift the cardboard box. Our ticket, the pattering of little feet inside sends my heart plummeting. "We're taking care of the problem, see? We'll be rid of her and life can go on as usual."

She narrows her eyes. "No it won't. Don't you get it? She's not feeding just on the misery we inflict, *she's feeding on ours.* She's going to destroy us. We'll never be the same."

"On ours?" I echo back to her.

Why didn't I realize that before? She's double dipping by making us do it. *It's tastier that way.* I should give Maven more credit. She's a genius right now for seeing between the lines, which have been drawn so clearly.

Maven stands a little bit straighter. "We're the only people who will know what happened here, assuming we make it through the next—crap!—less than forty-eight hours."

She's right, but I don't want her to be right. *Nothing will be the same*, I know that deep down, but I've been good at pretending my whole life. I look around, my mind searching for some kind of reasoning to continue pretending everything is manageable, to assume that life will go back to business as usual, the way it was before we booked that rental. I can't. If we survive, who's to say our friendship will, our sanity?

"So what? We blow everything up?" I ask.

She huffs. "I don't know, but I'm not going to be the same after this and if we do make it out, I'm not going back to the way things were."

The driver pulls up, taking us away from the tense conversation. "I can't do this right now. Let's just go." I motion to the car.

The drive back to the Airbnb is quiet, but I can't help but wonder what that really means. If she's never going back to how things were, should I do the same? How can I go on like usual when the most unusual thing possible is happening to us?

Maven looks out the window, refusing to look at me. I grip the cardboard box in my lap and the hamster has stilled. The little guy feels safe for now, but I don't. I know if we make it through this we'll never be the same, but what kind of future does that leave me with?

Pretending things are okay has gotten me this far in life, but I fear I'm nearing a dead end with that tactic. It's kept me safe, a *feeling* of safety at least—pushing anything too serious away. When anyone gets too close, I make it more casual. *Casual is comfortable.*

I've made a habit of finding shitty men and women who just want a fling, ways to fill the time because I know deep down that I'm damaged goods. I'm not made for the long-term. He made sure of that. He made sure to ruin me. For the longest time, I couldn't even be touched by another person, until I reclaimed my own body by putting a heavy armor over it and only taking it off if and when I choose. It's been a distant desire—a happily ever after, a maybe one day type of thing if the right person ever comes along. But I know for certain that will never be in my cards. Because I'll be the crazy lady who was haunted by a demon, a person haunted by the things she had to do. And no one would want that anymore than they want me now, once they really get to know me.

We walk up the creaky steps of the front porch, and I lock the door behind us with a hard click. I instantly feel stupid because our enemy isn't deterred by doors.

I don't know if hamsters scream and I hate that I have to consider that, so I go over to the radio on the adjacent kitchen bar top, turning it on while Maven goes to plop on the couch. The radio is playing some country station where the singer is talking about taking his truck down a dirt road, but that's all I process before I start to tune it out.

"What are you doing?" Maven asks from the sofa, tilting her head up to the ceiling.

"Don't ask."

"We need a plan." She positions herself upright. I assume what she means is *a hamster-killing-plan that's preferably merciful.* She searches for it for a moment. "What's something we can live with?"

"I'll do it." I hold a hand out as she tries to argue the responsibility. "It's my fault we're here in the first place and don't say that it's not. You'll probably hate me by the end of this if you don't already. Just let me make things right."

I'm the one who urged her to come up to the attic and I'm the one who talked her into doing the spirit board, so of course I can't help but feel guilty for the predicament we're in now. She opens her mouth then shuts it, confirming my thoughts.

"Christ," she says under her breath. She darts up from the sofa and stomps down the hall, moving right past me without looking back. She slams the bedroom door behind her.

I don't know exactly how, but I've made her upset. Regardless, she's feeling this way because of me.

I lightly tap on the door. "Mave, talk to me."

"Why, so you can dismiss me one more time? We're in this together, It doesn't matter how we got here, we're here. And just like everyone else around me, you want to cast me aside and call the shots."

I place my hand against the wood. "That's not it, I don't want to—"

"Just go away, Blair."

A part of me shatters. I've made a mess of this, of us. Though I'm trying my best, maybe my best isn't good enough, it never has been. And that's why I jump ship every time, but I'm not bailing on this one.

The hands on the clock floating on the wall sit at only 11:15, but I'm not carrying the doom of the chore around for the rest of the day, so I'll just get it done now and then I'll see if I can do something right.

I round the counter top, where I scan through the lower cabinets to find something heavy. My eyes settle on a cast iron skillet—the heavy ones you need two hands to grip upright. I let the heavy pan hang in my slack grip, and the cardboard crate clenched in my other fist. I wince when I look between the two objects I carry, but it needs to be done.

I'm backed into a corner, forced to make choices I wouldn't otherwise. We're here because of me. I need to do this. I planned the trip, it was me who wanted to seek adventure and bring Maven along with me. I pressured her into playing a game, just to prove we're not too old and stale, and now it may be the end of us all together.

I place one heavy foot in front of the other until I reach the door to the back patio. It's enclosed with a tall fence, granting complete privacy from the neighbors. All that's back here is a concrete slab with a hot tub positioned in the corner, a small patch of grass, and some potted plants. I place the box with a bite-sized heartbeat inside on the patch of grass. I haven't dared to look at the furry little thing since the pet store worker put it in there. It would make me second guess it and I can't do that. Our lives are more important, no matter what becomes of us next.

Raising the cast iron skillet, I hover it above the box with hands that shake with hesitation. Besides a fish—I don't feel like they count—I've never had a pet. This is technically my first one and I'm having to kill it.

Is it a pet if it doesn't have a name? I tell myself no and grip the skillet with a little more determination. Then I hear the door creak open behind me. Maven is standing there, watching.

"You can go back inside," I tell her. "You don't have to see it."

"I do. It's the first of three and you're not doing them all by yourself. I won't let you carry the guilt alone."

I turn my attention back to the box and drop the skillet with a force, flattening the box completely. There's a quick and faint squeak which makes my whole body recoil. I wait a moment to listen for any other sound, but hear none. Thank goodness. To do this twice would be torture. Except...I have to do this in some form or another two more times. And I'm not even sure if a small animal will cut it.

Lifting the pan, the flattened cardboard is stained with a small pool of bright red.

"Is it dead?" Maven asks from behind.

I peel back the layers to make sure. "It's dead." The question is now...did it work? Is the misery sufficient enough for her appetite? "So now I guess we just...wait?" I ask Maven.

She bites down on her lip, looking down at the blood stained cardboard. "I guess so. Do you want me to clean it up, since you...you know?"

I join her line of sight. Poor guy. He was just a pawn in a wicked game we don't want to play. "Doesn't matter."

She takes charge, grabbing the flattened mess and tossing it into the trash can next to the back door. "Problem solved."

Only if it were that easy.

A noise erupts from our left, making us both jump. The hot tub has turned on with the jets streaming. Lights display and bubbles charge. We look at one another with scrunched foreheads as if we're asking one another, *Did that just turn on by itself?*

I shrug. "Weirder things have happened."

Is it a signal Sasha's ready to talk about our offering? Well, if so, we may as well get comfortable.

Chapter 9

No Bikinis

Heat rises up to my face, prickling my skin with a warm spray of water. I sink down lower, hoping it will cleanse me—absolve me, if I'm lucky. This water won't renew me, but a girl can dream of a magical hot tub with those capabilities.

We left our tourmaline rings on the kitchen counter-top, a risky move. We can't ward her off any longer. We need to know the terms before we run out of time.

Maven sits across me in her light pink bikini, body toned thanks to her routine Pilates. I'm confident in my body, but my figure is credited to cigarettes and low protein which isn't the healthiest. I'm craving a cigarette more than ever right now and really regret not cashing in on that deal earlier. I wear a black one-piece with string laces down the plunging neckline. I thought it was a nice bathing suit, a little sexy but covered enough and in a color I tend to gravitate toward. But it looks like something Sasha would wear, and no matter how much of this color occupies my closet, I don't want any association with her.

She's obviously evil, but occupying my mind more than not and in a horrible way. So this may be the end of my relationship with the shade I feel best in.

I close my eyes to erase the thought of her, attempting to let it all melt away if only for a moment—yesterday, today, tomorrow.

The water sloshes as Maven moves closer. "What's the first thing you're doing when you get back?"

I let out a short chuckle. "Assuming we—"

"Humor me, Blair."

"I don't know. Definitely not buying a lottery ticket." I crack open my eyes. "Our luck is shit."

"I don't know about you, but after this, I won't be the same person anymore, B."

Moving to the middle of the hot tub, I sink down to my neck again. "Stop talking like that. We'll get through it. Things will go back to normal once she's gone." I lie to myself once more.

She squints at me like she's witnessed a betrayal. "Have I not spilled my soul to you? I'm *not happy* with the way things are." She lifts her arms up dramatically. "My life sucks, and I have no skills so I made a business being a fucking homemaker. I feel oppressed. We both may have been fine with pretending things are okay, but this is taking it too far, Blair."

I'm partly shocked because Maven rarely swears. And before she told me how unhappy she was, I wouldn't have known it was to this level because she's always been so good at looking content.

"Being a homemaker isn't exactly oppression, Mave, but I get what you're saying."

"And here I thought you were the feminist. Sure, being a home-maker isn't oppression, but it is when you have no other choice. I never got to go to college, like you. Matt never supported my education."

My eyes widen. She's absolutely right. "It was stupid of me to say. You should do what makes you happy, whatever that is. I can see it now." I move back to sit next to my best friend. She needs me—not the fun friend, but the friend who sticks by her through every hard thing. I need to be the friend she is for me. "When we get back, you should blow it all up. Live for you no matter what anyone else thinks. I'll support you every step of the way, I really mean that. I just wish I would have known sooner. I wish I would have *noticed* sooner."

"Don't. I'm good at pretending," she says.

We share a laugh that lacks humor. "Well that makes two of us."

She looks down at the flow of water. "There's something I haven't been telling you...it's because I was too embarrassed."

My heart rate increases. "What is it?"

"You asked me earlier what my reason was for being the way I am."

I hold out a hand to stop her. "No, we're not rehashing that. I didn't mean any of what I said."

"No. I need to get it off my chest," she says, shaking her head. "There's more to it." She pauses, then lets out a breath. "The truth is that he's been cheating on me for years, Blair. And I pretend I don't know." She looks at me with sad eyes. "That's what I've done with my life, stayed in a marriage I can't stand. And my reason? Because it's comfortable and I know nothing else."

I always knew Matt was selfish, that he treated her like a doormat, like a maid, and that Maven burdened it. But I never would have guessed he would stoop to that level. I surely can't imagine his logic. Any other woman would be a downgrade from Maven.

I blink a few times. "I didn't know...I never suspected it even." *Does that make me a shitty friend?* "Why didn't you ever tell me what was going on?" I ask.

"Because you would never tolerate that. You already hate him. I was too embarrassed to tell you, to tell anyone...I'm embarrassed now."

Tears beg to reach my own eyes. My best friend, since seventh grade, turned vegan, and has a cheating husband who she's only stayed with because he's *comfortable*—and I never knew.

"I just—I don't know who I am without it all—everything I built with Matt, but I don't want it anymore." She bites her lip, an attempt to control the admission about to escape. "None of it was what I ever wanted: the big house with an HOA, the country club membership, the Sunday brunches. It just happened because I let myself fit into the mold he wanted from me. Except for Junior; he was what I got right."

"You know I won't judge you. You've never judged me," I tell her. She raises her brow in response. "Okay you've never vocalized your judgement."

"No. You're right. I actually envied you," she admits.

"Bullshit. What is there from me to envy? I've floated through life, with nothing tying me down. I could die and it would take days for people to notice."

"You're everything I'm not. You do what you want, you're selfish, independent, and you don't care what anyone thinks. You never have."

"Well, I wasn't born that way; I was made to be that way. It's not all butterflies and rainbows. It's lonely, actually, being this way, creating space where no one else can fit." I splash water her way. "Except you. There's always been space for you."

She splashes back in defiance. "So you're telling me you still want to go back to a lonely apartment? You wouldn't change anything?"

"I guess I haven't thought that far ahead." An idea sparks. "Come with me, to New York or to London."

Her brows draw closer. "Seriously?"

"Yeah I'm serious. Remember how we used to talk about living together? It's not too late." I nudge her foot with mine.

I won't let her go back to a place where she's miserable. Is that hypocritical, though? I haven't made any declarations for change once this is over. Maybe Maven is braver than I am. I can't say I'm miserable, but I'm certainly not complete. I'm not sure if I ever will be.

"It could be too late," she says without a speck of confidence.

I don't know how to counter that because unless we play by these evil rules, that may be true. "If we don't want it to be, then it won't be," I tell her.

"Hmm. That's a simple statement with a complicated solution. Just promise me one thing?" she asks.

"What's that?"

"You'll meet me at the beach?"

I grab her hand. "No bikinis."

"No bikinis" stands as a promise that has kept us connected no matter how far apart we were in distance or life. Did I or do I still think it would really happen—that we'll make it to our dreamed up destination? If I'm being honest, no. But I still look forward to the ideal beach, where the past is never present and we can just be. Physically or metaphorically, we'll make it there, hand in hand. Maybe that's where we'll be complete.

The jets increase their pressure, bubbles churning, and steam rising. We back our bodies out of the water, sitting on the ledge of the hot tub with only the lower parts of our legs submerged. Placed there by some force of evil sorcery or Satan himself, Sasha is sitting across from us, wearing a simple bikini in her signature color. And just like before when I saw her body this bare, she looks fucking perfect. Water glistens on her skin, which is brighter and more human-looking today, like there's actually blood running through the veins underneath her skin suit.

"I'm not interrupting anything am I?" She scans us with a playful glint. "Are we skinny dipping?"

"No. We're not skinny dipping," Maven seethes.

Sasha eyes my body with the yellow irises she usually chooses to present with. "Too bad."

"So, I see you have your contacts back in," I say with more confidence than I should probably have.

She smirks. "Why? Did you like my other pair better?"

Why does she keep looking at me like that?

"Not particularly," I say past the lump in my throat. "Let's get the bullshit out of the way. Did it appease your appetite?"

I unearth the unavoidable question and bring it straight to her doorstep. Because if animals don't do the job, we have less than two days to make murder happen or seal our fate.

Sasha leans back, arms outstretched as she licks her upper lip, which is no longer chapped. They're quite glossy, actually. "For now. Thanks for the appetizer."

A heavy weight rolls off my shoulders, and Maven lets out a deep sigh.

"But I still require more," Sasha continues. "And next time, a furry little four-legged creature won't fill me up." I swear she flashes her eyes to black just to spite me. A smile curls up one side of her mouth. "Since you have some work to do, you should probably get dressed. Tick tock, ladies. You have approximately thirty-six hours."

We reluctantly get dressed to take on the rest of the day. Maven puts on the light blue sundress she had on earlier, pairing it with some white flats, and I get into a fresh set of clothes. My earlier set of clothes felt disgusting after doing what I did. Replacing them with a burgundy tank with dark jeans and my most comfortable red boots was a no brainer. If today ends the way I think it will, I may be scrubbing my entire body down instead of just changing clothes.

Sasha's waiting for us on the sofa. Neither of us are surprised by her presence at this point, we've gotten rather used to it I guess. I grab my ring off the kitchen counter, putting it in my purse while pulling my sunglasses out as a distraction. I position them on top of my head.

Sasha throws her head back in an effortless laugh and stands. She's dressed, too, in another black uniform to match the lack of humanity in her false body. She has knee-high black boots, skin-tight leather pants, and tank with the silver pentagram pendant reliably dangling.

"Dare we ask what's so funny?" Maven says, annoyed.

Sasha shifts her hip, resting one hand on it. "You two. That's what's funny." She eyes me up and down. "You look like if a haunted house and Nordstrom had a daughter." The comparison doesn't quite land. She looks at Maven. "And you look like you're about to go to brunch with your mother-in-law. Which is funny because she's dead."

"What's that supposed to mean?" I ask, unenthused.

"And since when does a demon go shopping at department stores?" Maven quips. I'm kind of surprised by her pointedness, it makes me stifle a small chuckle.

Sasha sends her an insulted look. "I get around." She switches her focus on me. "Oh. Nothing. Just that you dress up pretty only to scare people away. Are they running, or are you?"

I've never been insulted in such an odd and precise way.

"You don't know anything about me. And your snide comments aren't making me like you any more than I never did."

I don't know if she's grasping at straws while trying to hit a nerve, or if she really has some type of knowledgeable access to our inner sanctum. If that's the case, nothing is sacred. She's the last person—not even a person—the last being who I'd want to know what plagues me. She'd exploit it in a heartbeat, if she's not already.

How much exploitation is really necessary when you've been threatened with having your soul taken? I fear I'm about to find out.

"Au contraire. I know you don't want what you have now, neither of you do." Sasha strokes Maven's blonde, wavy hair, pushing it from her shoulder. Maven grabs her ring from the counter and holds it in front of her, making Sasha take a few steps back. "You're on a nowhere train and if you don't do what I ask, the train is going south for one of you." She smiles like she's envisioning our pleasant demise. "Way down south."

She gets a twisted pleasure in making us squirm, making us regret ever coming here, making us hate ourselves for what comes next. She laps up the misery like it's a puddle at our feet. I'm disgusted by what I see. She hides her true nature well, but I can see through the facade, I can see her enjoyment in our pain, how she thrives on it.

"You know, Hell really isn't that bad," she says. "We've got great lighting, high ceilings." She lets out a teasing laugh.

"I've already told you," I spout. "We'll do what you asked—if it gets rid of you."

I don't know how we'll get through the rest, other than one baby step at a time, but I do know what the threat is, and I don't want that for Maven. I don't want it for me. *I want to live.* I want to really live, to stop hiding and only giving morsels of myself to someone else. I haven't allowed anything too real, and neither has Maven. She deserves a full life, if not more than anyone does.

So we're doing this. No furry friends going forward, but a real sacrifice. A human sacrifice.

Chapter 10

Up in Smoke

The drink menu posted above the bar is in a ridiculously large font, but it helps since I forgot to put in my contacts this morning. If we're going down, and I mean that in a multitude of ways, I'm getting a drink first.

"I'll have a Bluebird," I tell the bartender.

"I don't care, just something strong that a non-frequent drinker can stomach," Maven tells the unfazed man with a towel draped over his shoulder.

I'm sure they get customers like us all the time. But we're not here for enjoyment, we're here to wash away the day, and to soothe an ache that's yet to come, which I'm hoping a few Bluebirds will ease. Alcohol is supposed to help you to lose your inhibitions, after all.

The bar isn't seedy, per say, but it's not a popular tourist attraction either. It's certainly not on any of the lists I put together. We were supposed to go to a bar that looked like a carousel, but that atmosphere just doesn't sit right anymore. We asked the Uber driver to bring us to a local favorite close by, and we ended up here, at *"Boudreux's."*

Instead of whimsy, there's darts, a pool table, and a dance floor with a small, empty stage next to it. There are a few retirees likely nursing their regular tonic and since it's the weekend, there's a handful of people our age and younger popping in and out.

The bartender brings us our drinks—mine in a martini glass, Maven's on the rocks—and we share the most un-enthused cheers to date. Maven takes a sip and makes a sour face, but then something in her expression changes and she rocks it back taking it all in two gulps.

She wipes her mouth with a napkin. "I'm hoping that kicks in soon. Bartender!" She raises her hand. "I'll take another."

"I guess that means I need to catch up." I take a few large gulps of mine, which isn't too hard. The liquor in this is well hidden. I nod to him. "Make that another for me too, please."

Reality feels a little lighter already.

A mildly attractive man somewhere probably in his twenties takes a seat next to Maven. He could be someone I wouldn't mind wasting time with, but he didn't take the seat next to me. Wait until he sees the wedding ring on her finger. You know, I actually don't think men look for that in this setting or they don't really care.

If I see a ring, I steer clear, unless I'm already too far gone to notice. If it's not me, it's just someone else anyways. I laugh to myself, realizing we probably have the same mindset, but mine takes way more liquor. It doesn't always make me feel good the next day, which is why I tend to steer clear. For now though, I have nothing better to do besides get reasonably drunk and observe.

His eyes focus on her finger while she downs her next drink. Maven sets the glass on the bar top and realizes there's someone next to her.

She turns to address the man who's been eyeing her. "Hi."

"Hi," he returns. "Here pretty early in the day, huh? I can't judge. I'm here, too."

"Well, there's been a rough start to it." Maven extends her hand, so formally. "Maven." She leans back, introducing me as well. "This is my friend, Blair." I give a tight-lipped smile and a wave.

He smiles back, amused by her as he takes in her beauty. He shakes her hand. "Ty. So where's your husband?"

Let's see how this plays out. One, he'll make a misogynistic judgment for her getting day drunk without her husband, or two, he'll take it as an opportunity, or three, he's just looking for conversation. I've seen all three before too many times.

Can't a woman go dancing with her friends or grab a drink without being under the thumb of a man? Going to a bar without your partner doesn't mean you're putting yourself on the market. We're here because we want to be. Well, I would prefer to be elsewhere, but we need the liquid courage today—not a good time.

Maven looks at her ring, holding her hand up and admiring the stone. "Hmm. That's a good question. My honest answer is that I don't really care where he is." She takes the ring off and drops it into her empty glass. *What. The. Fuck.*

"Hey, Mave. It may be the liquor talking," I whisper.

"It's not. You know it's not."

Ty sits back with a slight grimace. "Sorry. Didn't mean to trudge up a tough subject."

Maven smiles at him. "It's not even a subject anymore."

Who the hell is my friend right now? I mean, I can go with it. After what she admitted to me, I could only hope she would leave Matt. I just didn't expect her to make that decision in a bar, half drunk. But then again, the decision was made before now and is just accelerated by the circumstances we've found ourselves in.

Ty smiles back and pulls a piece of colorful paper from his back pocket. "Well in that case, you two should come to this party tomorrow night." He hands it to Maven.

"What kind of party?" I ask.

An older man further down the bar snickers with disgust. He's looking at Maven intently, blubbering something about whores and cheaters. If he only knew. It's not the first time a random man shares his unsolicited and uninformed decision, but for some reason it makes my blood boil.

"Damn whores," he mutters a little louder. This causes a head turn from our new friend, Ty.

"Hey, man. Be cool. You don't want to start any trouble here today. You know better than I do that they'll throw you out."

"I'll say what I want. They can throw me out." The old man points his finger at Maven. "It's whores like you that make men angry. Can't find a good woman anymore. You're all damn cheaters and liars."

The boiling anger inside of me has made its way to my face, and I'll bet if I looked in the mirror my cheeks would be beet red. I grip the stem of my empty glass. If it were hollow, I would have shattered it by now.

I clench my teeth. But why? Why hold my tongue when I could have my soul taken? It makes me smile a little, knowing I really don't give a flying fuck about holding my tongue against a sexist man. I've heard enough.

I lean over the counter so he can see me better. "I have a stellar idea. Why don't you shut the fuck up and go back to your beer? Your liver is probably begging for it."

He huffs and mutters some more vulgarities. Slamming his glass down, he takes a seat at a table across the bar so he doesn't have to look at us *whores* anymore. I'm guessing he's never got a taste of his own medicine.

Maven grabs my hand. "Blair..."

"He deserves worse than that. Don't pretend it's not true."

She shrugs and inspects the invitation with glowing neon colored letters. "A rave? I've never been to a rave."

"Ignore him," says Ty. "He's a drunk and he's in here all the time starting something." He offers a disarming smirk. "First time for everything then. If you come, find me. I'll be at the DJ booth."

Of course he's a DJ.

Maven nods. "We'll think about it. Thanks."

"Please do." He finishes his beer and closes his tab before standing, pulling a carton of smokes out of his pocket. "Either of you want a cigarette?"

Maven extends her hand. "Sure." Another surprise. I haven't seen this woman smoke a cigarette since we were fifteen. And she nearly coughed up her lungs.

"Why not," I agree, taking one from the carton. "Thanks."

He pulls out a lighter, flicking a flame for each of us. "Maybe I'll see you there." He offers a wink and then is gone.

We take a glance at the invite. "Wow. That's almost humorous," I say through a cloud of smoke. "When will we find the time? Between the second or the third sacrifice?"

I raise my hand to the bartender to get one last shot for us both. The inhibitions have proven to be lowered, but we'll need just a little bit more for what comes next.

"Right," Maven agrees, tucking the invite into her purse.

"We need a plan. Last drink then we have to get serious," I say to Maven. The bartender comes over. "One shot each please, then we'd like to close our tab."

"All right. Any ideas?" Maven asks.

I exhale a thick puff of smoke. "Not one."

Maven lets her cigarette simmer between her fingers, ash collecting on the tip while I take several non-cleansing inhales. There's a twinge in her brow. "What was that? You were thinking something."

She shakes her head. "Nothing."

"Not nothing. Anything is on the table right now. If we don't come to a conclusion, the decision will be made for us." I press one more time. "What were you thinking?"

She looks around. The bartender is coming closer to give us our shots, short glasses with the last little bit of courage necessary. We pause our plans, shoulders tense, until he's out of earshot again.

"Cheers." Maven clinks her small glass with mine and we down it. "It was just an idea," she whispers as she places her empty glass back down.

I lean in closer. "Let's hear it."

"Matt's Mom was in a palliative care unit in the last stage of her cancer. It's basically a place where people go to die."

"That's actually not a bad idea." I let out a shameful sigh and we share a perturbed look. "Listen, I know. I don't want to either, but Mave, that may be like the best idea we have." She cocks her head with a soft shake in defiance. "Don't make me the bad guy here, Mave. We *have* to choose someone." I look down, ashamed for what I'm about to say. "It's them or us. Do you want to die? Because I don't."

"I know. I know. Fuck!" She takes a long drag from her cigarette now, like she needs it now more than ever, followed by a violent coughing fit, which garners a couple of looks.

I keep my voice small. "We can find someone there who's almost dead. It won't be like we're killing them, not really." That's what I'm telling myself at least.

Her eyes are watered and red, but she catches her breath. "No. I don't want to die, I'm just not sure I'm willing to make someone else pay the price for that. But if it's the best we can do, we have to at least try."

That's the difference between me and her. I *am* willing to have someone else pay the price for my own life, anyone but Maven. I may not have known that before, but I do now under the pressure. She's pure, she's deserving, she didn't ask for this. She hasn't even had the chance to live her life according to her own choosing. I also realize, here and now, that in the off chance we can't deliver, I'd pay that price for her.

I pull up the nearest hospital on my phone. "It's a plan. I'll order a ride." It feels like all humanity is gone from both of us, but if I call any attention to it we may fold, so I put it out of mind.

I'm not killing someone. I'm saving us.

She pulls her phone out and starts typing.

I peek over. "What are you doing?"

She sniffles, fingers dancing on the screen. "A final goodbye, for Junior. When this comes to a close I want him to know how proud I am of him, how much I love him. And my sanity is deteriorating by the hour, so I better say it now."

I grip her arm. "We'll get through this, Mave. I promise. Just go through the motions. No more talk of what's right and wrong, we've decided. We're surviving this, right?"

She nods. "Right." It's not convincing, but I don't need convincing, I need compliance. She gets up off her stool. "I'm going to the bathroom." She walks down the dim hallway to the restroom, a small cloud of smoke puffing behind her steps.

If Sasha is truly feeding on our misery, plus the act itself, she's about to get it buffet style.

I wait for Maven on the curb after closing our tab, no one knowing what we're going through but us. People walk past and I wonder if any of them are secretly suffering from a haunting they can't tell anyone about. *How many people has she done this to?*

I play out the process in my head. *We'll walk in, say we're visiting a family member—hopefully convincingly enough to get in. If the security is tight, we're screwed. How will we do it? Smothering takes minutes, so I've heard, but it has to be the least detectable method, right? These people are probably low on oxygen to begin with. We'll have to give fake names, too.*

Maven exits the bar, pulling me from my anxiety-riddled thoughts. "What are you thinking?" she asks.

"How to commit murder." I take one more drag and drop my smoke on the ground, crushing it under my boot. "Don't worry about the details, okay? I've got a plan."

Chapter 11

Casualty

It smells like some sterile solution in here, not one I can name by any other than *"hospital smell."* As we roam the halls to the upper floor where the Grim Reaper makes his rounds, the halls are emptier, quieter, and more ominous. It almost feels abandoned. Shouldn't there be nurses or something walking around?

I've always hated hospitals without really knowing why, but it's clearer as I wind these empty passages that they're sentinels of death and disease. And we're at the epicenter.

The arrows on the walls lead us into what feels like a never-ending maze. I grip the small arrangement I picked up in the gift shop below, water sloshing back and forth. It's not like we're itching to get there, so we walk slowly, the flowers slightly masking the scent of medical grade cleaner they mop the floors with. We haven't spoken a word since the driver picked us up from the bar. Not much to speak of, really. If we did, we may talk ourselves out of it. So silence is preferred.

Maven sighs. "I know you said not to worry about the details, but I'm in this just as much as you are, so I need to know...the details, I guess."

Despite the several drinks, my throat throbs with a dryness. "It's better if you don't know, just go along with it. It will be easy. And I'm not counting you out. I just don't want you to panic."

I don't think any form of death is easy, but I hope a pillow over the face of someone who already has trouble breathing doesn't take more than a couple of minutes. I'm sure as hell not gonna do an internet search and leave an obvious trail back to me.

This will be the perfect murder. Random. No connection. We're travelers. These are thoughts I never imagined would cross my mind, but here I am. Oh how things change when not just your life, but your best friend's life, and both your souls are on the line.

The reception desk comes into view. "I guess this is it huh?" Maven says. "No turning back."

"No turning back." I keep my eyes forward. "We don't have a choice," I remind us both.

"I know." She urgently nods her head, forcing herself to believe it. "Our hands are basically forced."

"Yeah. Basically," I echo. "The blood's not on our hands, it's on hers."

There's a nurse stationed at the long desk with thin-rimmed glasses, scrolling away on her phone. My heart threatens to beat right out of my chest, but I take the lead. With each step that leads closer, my heart pounds heavier. Sweat builds in various places, but I manage to hold myself together. We just need to make it past the desk without being noticed because we don't know who we're visiting, and we have no name to give. I look behind me, passing Mave a glance that says, *"Follow my lead."*

We walk right past the desk. The nurse seems too caught up in her social media feed to notice, at least I hope so. *Keep looking forward.* Rounding the corner, an empty, stale, dead-end hallway waits for us.

At the face of the hallway is an old, framed stock photo of a sandy beach sunset. It's probably been there since the 90s. It taunts me with the ideal vacation glow to nowhere. *There's nowhere to run*, it says. *You're about to commit murder and the only way out is past that desk again, so welcome. Come see if you win or lose.*

It's not a game for me. It may be for Sasha, but if I lose this game, I could lose my life. So losing is not on the table. I already decided that. This won't be the last beach sunset I see, and this dead end is nothing but an obstacle. One I'll knock down.

We continue down the dated hallway with salmon-colored tiles on the perimeter—an unsightly decor choice. With slow steps, I peer into the first room, passing it as unassuming as possible. Nothing and no one's in there, except an empty bed that's either recently emptied or soon to be filled.

In the next doorway we pass, there's a man sitting up, barely awake—but awake enough—and watching a sports game from the sounds of it. I bite the inside of my cheek, knowing we'll deliver a grim fate to someone in one of these rooms.

It's not an idea anymore, it's a solution to a problem, here and now.

In the third room we pass, there's a woman laying motionless in a bed, wearing an oxygen mask. Her eyes are closed and she already looks moribund. Fuck me, but fucking bingo.

"This one," I whisper. Maven nods, following me in.

She grabs hold of my arm, clutching onto it like we're walking through a haunted house and I'm her anchor to safety. I don't know what delusion I've cultivated, but I'm no source of safety. I'm a beacon for whatever Sasha is. She probably saw me and knew I was someone she could sink her nasty claws into.

"Is she sleeping?" Maven asks.

I make my way closer to the bed with each hesitant step. The woman's chest barely rises and falls, and her eyes stay shut. Her gray hair, wiry and wild, sprouts like coiled roots on the white pillowcase under her frail, liver-spotted head.

The flowers I hold were a buffer, an excuse to have in the unfortunate event she were awake. In that case, I would lie about being here to spread some joy.

I gently place the small vase of carnations and daisies on the counter close by. She's fallen asleep to the local news channel, the noise filling the blank space. I guess that's one of the few things these people who are essentially bed-ridden and waiting for death have to do. They spend their days watching what the rest of the world is doing.

A weird feeling washes over me. I can't name it, but it's not guilt. *Who wants to live like this?* In some sick way, I feel I may be doing her justice.

"What now?" Maven pulls me out of my introspection.

I motion to the oxygen machine next to her bed. My murder weapon—a little knob that feels so removed.

"You need to take her off the monitor first," Maven whispers.

Right. Once I turn it and her vitals start diminishing, lights and alarms will flash to alert nurses to the room. At the perfect moment to use my true crime consumption to my benefit, I don't. I understand *why* and *how* killers are so reckless. Because when you're actually here, when you're desperate and your mind is racing, it all falls out the window.

"I don't know where to start," I admit. "What switch do I flip or what plug do I yank?"

"I'll do it," Maven says, looking at me with an enormous serving of sorrow, like she's being forced to commit the most atrocious crime. Because she is. *We are.*

She presses a button on the monitor, causing the screen to go black. Onto the next step. The news channel anchor is echoing behind me, but I can't tell you a single thing they're saying. Noise drowns out and the task ahead is all I can see or hear.

I touch the knob on the oxygen tank. A little black knob—a small twist is all that stands between me and my soul's fate. If she wakes up, I'll grab the pillow and make it quick. I crank the knob, watching the little dial flutter down, down, down.

The woman doesn't move, she looks like she's already dead. Her eyelids, thin with little blue veins visible through her paper thin skin, stay sealed. Her mouth is slightly opened under the oxygen mask. As her oxygen lowers, she doesn't even make a sound. Maybe she's been given a sedative. For both our sakes, I hope so.

Maven gasps and I whip my head in her direction. Her attention is on the TV.

"What?" I whisper harshly.

She points up at the screen with a horrified look. "I did that. That was my fault. It was me."

With my hand still on the knob, I hear the voice of the news anchor.

"Live on the scene, we have word from the fire chief, the fire originated from the women's bathroom. They say there was one casualty, no others injured. We do not have the name of the deceased, but our prayers are with them and their family. This was a tragedy today, but first responders say they were able to put out the fire before it reached the rest of the building."

Holy. Fucking. Shit. On the screen is a live view of the bar we were just at. Smoke billows behind the anchor, black soot scarring a section of the wall. *One casualty.*

A little spark of something lights inside me. "What do you mean, it was you?" I ask Maven.

She stands there, motionless, eyes glued to the screen. I wave my hand in front of her face. "Mave."

She pries her eyes away, they're rimmed with water. "The cigarette. I tossed it in the trash can like an idiot."

Of course she did. She doesn't usually smoke, her mind was jumbled, she was buzzed, and she didn't know it would start a fire.

I grab her shoulders. "Mave. Do you know what this means?" I grin from ear to ear.

She looks disgusted, and I recoil at the look she gives me. "I killed a man. That's what it means." An awareness becomes her, and she turns to the frail skeleton that was once a woman filled with life. "What are we doing?"

She goes over to the oxygen tank, reaching for it.

"Stop!" I seethe, though my voice still at a whisper.

With one of her hands on the knob, she says, "We're better than this."

"Maybe I'm not," I warn her. "Get your hand off of that knob. It's already done! This one's not on you. I'm the one that turned it."

"But you are better than this." Her chin trembles.

She's wrong. I'm not.

"This would be the last one, Mave. It would be over if we just let it happen." I plead, but she turns the oxygen back up.

My head hangs and my hope falters.

"It's not right," she cries. Her cries start to get louder, and the old woman becomes unsettled by the noise. She hasn't moved an inch since we walked in here, but a cry wakes her?

"Maven! Not here, you'll wake her up."

She darts out of the room. I throw my head back. We were so close to this being over. I have two options right now: follow her because I don't know where the hell her head is and where she's running off to, or I could turn that little dial back down.

Chapter 12

Tick Tock

I made a choice. It may cost me—cost us—but I couldn't leave Maven alone, not with what she's struggling to process right now. I don't know what it feels like to kill someone, but Maven does. And she's in the belly of it right now.

I caught up to her, though she made no attempt to slow down as I called for her through the halls of the hospital. We sit on a park bench one block away, in silence, panting. I want to glare at her, tell her she ruined it, but I can't. She's hurting.

Folded over, head in her hands, she rocks. I've never seen her like this, but then again there are a lot of new things I've witnessed over the past couple of days. Seeing her like this hurts all the same.

I place my hand on her back. "It's okay."

"No. It's. Not," she says through quick breaths.

"It wasn't intentional," I tell her, attempting to cushion the impact. "It's a good thing depending on how you look at it."

She shoots herself upright. "A good thing?" Snot drips from her nose. "Nothing that's happened since we got here has been a good thing."

I can't win. But I'll happily accept the role of the bad guy to get us where we need to be if that's what it takes. I clench my fists.

"What am I supposed to say? I don't even know what the right thing to say would be...other than we're in an impossible spot and that could have just made things easier." I may regret saying this, but she needs to hear it. "I do think it's a good thing. An even better thing if it was that misogynistic asshole who got sacrificed."

Though I love it about her, Maven's goodness is not helpful right now. No matter the impossible, she maintains it, her humanity, her nature. Is this my nature that I've had all along—self preservation, or is it a newly developed trait? If I can develop it, will Maven ever be able to? I'm not sure, so I'm taking the lead here.

I grab her hand to take the ring off her finger without asking. She pulls back, but I already have it in my grasp. I twist it away.

"What are you doing?" she cries out.

"Just trust me." I put the ring in my purse along with mine and toss the purse by its strap. I need her here. I need to know if it counts.

A tissue floats between us in mid-air, held by a hand with black-painted nails. Maven snatches it away without addressing Sasha's presence and wipes her nose with it.

"You're welcome," Sasha says.

She looks even more radiant now. Her skin glows with a healthy radiance, her dark hair is fuller with a bouncy shine, and her lips are a brighter shade. It would appear she doesn't need a spa day to revitalize her image, but something deadlier. She stands confidently, giving me an up-and-down as usual. Her eyes finally settle on mine. The way she looks at me is like she knows a secret I haven't told anyone but her or like she wants to eat me alive. I can't decide between the two.

"Not just for the tissue," she quips to Maven, switching her gaze in her direction. "You're friend was almost right. While not intentional on your part, it was still you who caused his death." Sasha looks at me. "The misogynistic asshole."

"So it counts?" I ask.

"I may have locked a door, but yes. It counts." She winks. Maven stays seated on the park bench, gently rocking forward and back. "You don't look too happy though?" Sasha points out with a raised brow.

"Leave her alone," I tell her.

Sasha cocks her head to the side. "Why? Isn't it her fault you're not rid of me already? Or do you just like my company?" She wears an awfully sexy smirk as she says it. "You almost had it up there—"

"Stop!" I press my eyes shut in frustration. "She stopped me from doing something I would regret."

Sasha's mouth parts like she's about to try and prove me wrong. There's a mix of disbelief and amusement painting her face that instantly heats my body with annoyance. "Are you sure about that?" she finally asks.

"You can't force us to be who you want to make us into!" Maven shouts, spinning around. "You're vile, evil, blood-thirsty, but I would rather *die* than stoop to your level!"

Sasha blinks, unfazed and leans her elbows onto the back of the park bench. "Don't you know? There's been no forcing. Everything you've done and will do, is of your own volition. If you would rather die, *then die*." She leans closer to Maven's ear, but looks at me when she speaks. "I've never forced a hand, Blondie, only encouraged what's always been there."

Maven tenses. "We're nothing like you."

"Let me show you something first and then you can decide, hmm?" Sasha grabs Maven's hand and offers hers out to me. I hesitantly grab hold.

As soon as I touch her hand, I become weak in the legs. My eyes roll back into my head, a feeling similar to falling asleep, except once I regain clarity I'm awake and somewhere new. We're in a cold, white hallway. It looks like another hospital.

"Where did you take us?" I ask.

Sasha walks ahead, summoning us with the wave of her finger. "Follow me."

Maven and I keep close, following Sasha down the stark white hall with an ominous chill and no end in sight. We pass thick metal doors with small square windows at eye-level. I don't dare question what's on the other side of them.

"Mommy's home," Sasha echoes.

Screams erupt while dread consumes me. Their shrill sounds of terror violate my ears.

I shudder. "What is this place, Hell?"

She stops at a door and reaches for the knob. "If it was, you wouldn't have to ask. This is still the real world, but this hallway"—she looks around—"I like to refer to it as my *collection*." Time stops and every hair on my body stands at attention. *Her collection?* She turns the bulky knob. "Come see."

"I'd rather not."

"Why? It's your destiny after all. Unless you comply."

"What's on the other side of the door?" Maven presses.

"Nothing compared to what's below." Sasha flashes a smile. "I like to keep my souls pretty and earthbound—part time, at least. Behind the door is just a girl, like you." She reaches for Maven's face, caressing it. "One who thought she was too good for me. Who just wanted to be *so good*, above all else."

She opens the door and we peer inside to see a shell of a woman, pretty but vacant. She sits on the thin, rusted metal bed—the only thing occupying the room she's locked in. She doesn't even acknowledge our presence.

"Can she see us?" I ask.

"Of course she can," Sasha says. "She just doesn't care anymore. She refused to give me what I wanted, so she's mine now."

The woman rocks back and forth, her white gown stained and her auburn hair tangled. Sasha sits behind her and the bed creaks under the extra weight. Once more, the woman does nothing more than accept where she is and what's happening. Sasha produces a hairbrush, moves the hair from her face to her back and begins brushing.

"If you would have it your way, if you decide my level is too low for you to stoop"—Sasha looks at Maven with the most seriousness she's displayed yet—"consider this room yours."

Sasha begins braiding her hair into a single braid down her back, while we just stand and watch because there's nowhere else to go. Here, we're at her mercy. I grasp Maven's hand tightly. What's stopping her from just trapping us here? She could.

The woman quickly rises to her feet, then screams, clawing at her hair and making a ruffled mess of the braid. Maven and I both back up to the wall, fearful she'll claw at us too.

Sasha makes a sour face. "She doesn't appreciate my help as much as she used to. Oh well." She gets up and offers both of her hands out to us, palms up. I take it greedily, while the woman sinks into the corner and lets out another ear-piercing scream.

Sasha brings us back to the park bench and my vision adjusts. "What do you say, Blondie?" Sasha asks. "Still willing to become her?"

Maven keeps her face stoic, like a saint. "I won't kill anyone else."

Bile rises within me. *She would rather die.* My chest caves at the thought. I don't want that to be true, but if she admits it in the face of doom, it must be her honest answer. I know what's going to happen this time, and I finally know how it's going to end. Sasha will take one of us as promised.

And it will be me. *I'll make it me.*

Someone like Maven doesn't deserve that fate, but I might. I was willing to kill. I value my life above someone else's, so what if I have turned into something of Sasha's making? What if she really did just unearth something in me that always was? If that's the case, my soul isn't waiting to be tainted, she's already in me.

"You won't end up like her, Mave." I kneel in front of the bench, my hands on her trembling legs. "If I can do one thing right, it's this." My eyes dart up to Sasha. "Take me."

Sasha crosses her arms and arches a brow. "Really, you would do that—offer yourself to me?"

"I would."

She looks down at Maven like she's a pathetic little thing, curling her lip ever so slightly in utter disappointment, then at me with the same expression. She takes a deep, resetting inhale, relaxing her shoulders. "Well, the clock is still ticking. In case you change your mind." She winks at me, then fades away.

"She's gone," I say. Maven's breathing has steadied, but she hasn't said a word yet. "What are you thinking?"

She closes her eyes and shakes her head. "I can't let you do that. You can't just offer yourself in my place."

"Well guess what? I'm your stubborn best friend who won't let you make all the choices today."

She holds my face in her hands. "If you go, I go. I won't let you go to that place alone."

My nose burns and tears form waiting to fall. It was always us. Then life happened—her responsibilities, me running away from what one could call responsibilities, distance, her shitty husband, our shitty life choices in general. I love her more than anyone else, my platonic soul-mate.

A heavy tear makes its way down my cheek and travels down my chin. "Okay then. Together."

She wipes my tears. "Together."

"We have tonight and one more day," I tell her. "So let's get our asses up and go live."

There are pools of understanding in her own eyes, tears already painting her cheeks. She laughs. "It's really over, isn't it?"

"One way or another, yeah." I get up, joining her side at the bench as we hold one another's hands, staring into the sunset in silence as if it could be one of our lasts.

I feel it in my chest that our lives are over. Sasha gave us no rule book or contract to refer to. Will I spend the rest of my years in some asylum, another one of her dolls added to a collection of souls until I drop dead? Is my soul damned to Hell? Whatever happens, it's happening, I've chosen it.

I look in the direction of the hospital. Our ticket was right there. It would have been so easy, it felt easy, but then again it didn't.

I was turning into the monster Sasha wanted me to be when I turned that knob and my remorse faded away like steam rising from a cup, dissipating into nothingness. That woman was dying and I didn't care. I convinced myself I would be doing her a service. I convinced myself it would be a kind thing to do. But as sick and twisted as it is, I still believe it.

Sick and twisted, that's what I almost was to Maven. To have my image formed into something gnarled and unrecognizable to her would crush me. The look in her eyes when I was trying to convince her of murder almost ruined me. Is it crazy that I would rather go there, to the room with a rusted bed and no hope, than to do that? Rather than to let something take away my autonomy and mold me into a form Maven is disgusted by?

If that woman died at my hand, sure we may have gotten out of this, but not without scars. Would we part ways and try to forget this ever happened? Would we ever speak again? Would she have hated me?

Maven dries her eyes with the handkerchief Sasha gave her. "Well this is way overdue, but given the circumstance, I guess there's no time like the present." I watch her pull out her phone and call Matt's number.

"What are you doing? You're not going to tell him anything are you?" She doesn't respond to me, just waits while the phone is pressed to her ear. "Mave!" I clench my jaw.

She keeps her emotion unreadable. What the hell could she be needing to call him for? I haven't thought about calling anyone for the past two days, in fear Sasha may decide to swing by and cause me to say something that earns me a ticket to the asylum.

He answers. I'm unsure what he's saying because all I can hear is Maven.

I swear I see a smile slip onto her mouth when she utters the words, "I'm not coming back."

I'm speechless. It's a nail in the coffin for her marriage. To talk about it is one thing, to do it is to basically go ahead and start engraving our headstones.

She stays stoic, showing no crushing emotion. How could there be when her marriage has been nothing but a matter of convenience?

"I'm done being your doormat," she bites out. "I really should have left you a long time ago. Have the life you deserve, Matthew." She ends the call. Despite the doom that awaits us, there's a small pebble that falls away from the boulder overhead.

"How did that feel?"

"Amazing," she breathes out. "Like I reclaimed a part of me back, a part he stole a long time ago. It's too bad I won't get to enjoy my new freedom, but as long as I spend what remaining time I have left with you, I'll be okay." She grabs my hand, squeezing it.

Reclaiming a part that was stolen—I know that feeling too well. Maybe I did it in all the wrong ways, but I have no regrets. When my innocence, my choice, my autonomy was taken, it was merely a game, one in which he won. I won't utter his name. No one believed me besides Maven and Mom, though over the years, I've realized that's all I needed anyway. He got away and probably continued to hurt other girls.

Fifteen—that's how old I was when my youth pastor took advantage of me. That's how old I was when I realized men can't be trusted. And then I hardened.

I try my hardest not to ever revisit that summer. But sometimes, late at night, it creeps back in. Youth camp, 2004. It was hot and sticky and we were laying down sod for a family whose house had just burnt down. It felt like a good thing was being done, but I ended up scorched just like the earth under the grass I was helping lay. The youth group was rewarded with a cabin stay at the state park close by, where we were meant to relax and enjoy time spent with our friends. I didn't have a sharp tongue or the backbone I needed back then; I was just a kid. Dirt under my fingernails, salty with sweat and soaked in chlorine, he cornered me in the pool showers and claimed no one would believe me if I told anyone. And he was mostly right.

Maybe I won't have a story-book romance like others dream of. No one gets the chance to hurt me, but no one gets the chance to love me either. I've sacrificed one for the other.

The church faculty, congregation, my own Dad even, refused to believe the youth pastor was capable of being the monster I knew him to be. Running away to New York seemed like the answer. I can hardly be around Dad anymore because when I look at him, I see the monster he chose to believe over me. Unfortunately, Mom pays for his indiscretion by seeing me only once a year.

For her to stand by him after he turned his back on me was almost enough to make me never want to come back again. On the other hand, my anchor, Maven, never strayed far from our hometown. Over time I understood, while I can't relate, why Mom chose to stay. She never had any independence—something my mother and Maven shared until recently—so I made sure I never had to depend on anyone. Instead, I built a life where I could get by just fine by myself. Now I'm not so sure how happy I am that's the path I chose.

But is anyone really prepared for the end? What to do with life never seemed so serious, so urgent until now. I've fed the flesh, and made smart financial decisions, so in that instance I didn't miss out, but the other things—the things that people search for and few find, I have a hint of regret about never really giving it a worthwhile shot.

I grab my purse from the bushes. "What should we do with what we have left?" I ask.

Maven nudges my arm. "I have an idea. But first, I have something I want to do."

Charred brick, exposed beams and partial ruins make up the old bar, still accompanied by a few firemen and yellow tape.

"I feel horrible," she says.

"You know she accelerated this, right? You can't blame yourself for the death she caused."

She says nothing. We just watch, perched on the curb across the street. The smell of smoke consumes the air and the sidewalk is still wet from putting out the flames.

"He probably had a family," she goes on.

"So do you." I can't help myself, but I immediately regret saying it. A reminder of all we have to lose is not what we need right now. Especially if we've chosen not to do the one thing that could get us out of this situation.

"I'm a Christian, Blair. I can't in good conscience kill someone for my own greed. I'm sorry if I disappointed you."

"Then where are our guardian angels? Where is God himself?"

"It's not the best time to question religion," she returns.

I'm glad one of us has some optimism left. I want to say, *"It might be the perfect time, actually."* Because my faith has left the room at this point, but I won't diminish hers any further.

Like an omen with perfect timing, Sasha appears in front of us, back facing us. Our reliable dark cloud views her destruction from the middle of the street. "Killers always return to the scene of the crime." She looks back over her shoulder. "Been guilty of it a time or two myself."

"I won't indulge you," Maven says weakly.

Sasha spins on her heel. "And I only came here to tell you I won't bother you anymore if you've made your choice. I just thought you should know he murdered his first wife and got away with it." The admission startles me. This gets Maven's attention as well as mine. She gauges our reactions. "In some way you could call it justice."

"How would you know that?" I ask sharply.

"Demons know things," Sasha returns. "Things no one knows." She crouches down in front of me and presses a gentle finger to my forehead. "Things that stay up here. And maybe, just maybe, I'm more of an altruistic demon than you may think."

There's an allure to her. Maven doesn't see it. But I watch the form Sasha chose from where I sit on the curb. I take in her dark beauty, sense the subtle sweetness that laces her words and the intention behind them. I wonder if, very deep under there somewhere, there's another side we don't see? A side that demons aren't supposed to have.

Chapter 13

Killers

The racy clothing boutique we passed yesterday still has the pink neon sign set aglow—*The Shimmer Shack*. It's filled with versions of ourselves we never would've dreamed of becoming. It was Maven's idea, but I can't think of a better way to wrap this mess into a bow than by doing something fun and a little reckless with her by my side.

There's stretchy tops and bottoms with cut-outs and mesh, platform shoes covered in sparkles, booty shorts with fringes, and bras with spikes—a plethora of people we can be. I don't really feel like me and I don't think Maven does either. If she did, we wouldn't be here. There's no going back, so perceptions aside, we're just going to lap up the rest of what life has to offer.

Maven's mood has changed now that she knows the man she had help with killing may have actually deserved it. And we've accepted our fates, or are putting brave faces on at the least. We're going out together and we're going out in style. I never thought a rave is where I would end this life.

The boutique closes in one hour, so I grab for things without much consideration. I hold a few outfits in my hands while waiting for Maven to come out of the single dressing room, which is a curtain in the corner of the store. She moves the shimmering sequined fabric to one side, stepping out in full attire. I've seen her naked before, as all best friends have, but this is the most skin I've seen her show in, well, forever. My jaw drops.

She spins and the reflective pink fabric shimmers as she does. Her bra top crosses at the front, haltering around her neck, showcasing an impeccable set of tits—something I wasn't gifted with but if I had been, I would wear that. Her bottoms are cheeky with a ruched ultra mini that joins on one side. Underneath it are neon-green thigh-high fish-nets that go down to reflective platform boots. She looks like a Barbie on acid.

"You look..."

"Different?" she asks.

"I was going to say hot, like arson-level hot."

The color almost drains from her face but then she bursts into a fit of laughter, an uncontrollable one. "Your humor has always been dark, but damn. I think you deserve an award for that one."

"Yeah that one was kind of far, even for me, but I figured I'm going to say what's on my mind for the rest of my time. No holding back, right?"

That's the promise we made on the way here: no holding back. Anything we want, any experience we want, we'll have with no judgment from the other.

Maven gestures to the changing room, trading places with me. "I'm not sure I can top arson-level hot, so it's your turn."

I come out in black booty shorts and a cropped long sleeve with sporadic cut-outs everywhere. Oval cut-outs run down the middle of the chest, with smaller ones on the sides and all over the arms. The sleeves go down to my hands, looping around my thumbs. Black garters with silver hearts in their center hug my thighs, and black platform sneakers finish the look. I said I wanted to part with black, but it feels natural, and I'm not letting Sasha take that away from me. I know I'm nothing like her, I still have my humanity—if I didn't we wouldn't be where we are, on the edge of death.

"You look killer." Maven nods. "It's criminal, really." We stand arm in arm, facing the mirror, polar opposites, but somehow fused. "You know, this is actually how I thought it would be at one point."

"How what would be?"

"Us. Not like this, but you and me. That we would grow old and gray, you and I would move in together and live out the rest of our days as sassy old biddies, then die on the same day." She smiles at me like it's not one of the most twisted things she's ever said. Still, it's also the sweetest.

I bump her with my hip. "Me too."

We may not have had the same vision, but I always thought, somewhere deep down, that life would be better together, that it would make sense that way.

I never had a child or husband to come home to, so I created my own things to come home to: a glass of wine, work, an empty bed that would occasionally host a visitor.

I mean, all best friends dream of living together, going off to college, and renting a place for a few years—that in between of adolescence and adulthood where you're lost but you have someone to be lost with. My ideal life didn't end there, and it didn't begin as sassy old women.

I never wanted a husband, really, I mostly just wanted my freedom. And I guess I got that in New York, but one thing always missing was her, and not in a "secretly in love" way, but like she's another part of me. Maven is the only one I let in. I guess if neither of us are getting to live out our dream, we can at least enjoy what we have left with each other. There has to be some comfort in that.

We change out of our clothes because I am not walking the streets of the French Quarter so exposed. I go to the cashier to get our things rung up.

"Where are you two taking these outfits? Got anything fun planned?" the cashier asks.

Maven tucks her wallet back into her purse. "We're going to a rave tomorrow night. I think the invitation said *"Acid House."*

The cashier folds the clothing into tissue paper before placing it in a bag. "Oh. I've been to one of those."

I can hear something behind her tone that doesn't sit well. "What did you think of it?" I ask.

She presses her lips together and looks at me with curiosity. "Is this your first?"

"It is."

She slips the last piece of the clothing into the bag. "Just be careful. Sometimes people will give you something and it's laced. I play it safe and bring my own."

"Drugs?" Maven asks.

The cashier smiles. "Yeah. I prefer hallucinogens, but everyone enjoys it differently. It's just not always safe to take from people you don't know." She pushes the boxes and bags toward us. "Don't let me scare you, though. It's still a lot of fun. Raver life and festivals get a bad rep because of people like that. You two seem smart."

"Thanks for the tip," I tell her.

I open the hatch door to the rental car we went back for earlier, setting our stuff inside. "Plan on partaking?" I ask Maven.

"Why not?" she says. "I haven't tried anything before, may as well indulge while we can, right?"

"Yeah I think it would be fun. Indulgence. I can get with that."

It's a short drive back to the Airbnb. As much as I want to say I feel okay with what's happening because we're together, I'm not. Sequins, shimmer, drugs, and alcohol can only take the edge off for so long.

There's a heaviness lingering in my chest—a feeling of doom. Because I don't know what waits when the timer runs out. I don't know how long I have before I'm stuck in that cold, stale place, with no warmth, no hope, just misery. I grip the leather wrapped steering wheel and try to push it down, deeper into my consciousness, when Maven makes another surprising statement.

"I want a burger. A fat, greasy one."

I cut her side eye. "Say no more. I was curious how long that would stick."

Leaving the fast-food drive-through, she stuffs her face—basically inhaling a double cheeseburger with all the fixings. "You know, it was never my idea in the first place. I just did it because it made him happy. How pathetic is that?" Sauce dribbles on her chin.

"Does it taste as good as you remembered? And it's not pathetic, it's...okay maybe a little pathetic."

She throws a French fry at me as we laugh. "And yes. It tastes better than I remember, actually."

We arrive back to where this all started—the little, charming and unassuming pink shotgun house with teal shutters like no other. In the evening glow, it looks even more inviting, but it's not—not really, though the effort has surely been applied. The closer I look at it, the skillful facade becomes more noticeable. A cold sweat comes over me. Freshly tended shrubbery borders the porch and two potted plants are placed on either side of the entrance. The fresh coat of bright paint, and a welcoming wreath hanging on the front door camouflages the beast inside. These upgrades make me suspect it all to be intentional—either by the owner or Sasha.

Did she choose this house or did the house choose her?

"I'm so tired," Maven admits in an exhausting breath.

I kick off my shoes. "Me too." I'm not sure how we could possibly get a restful sleep, but we can try. Then, I remember something our Uber driver, Jaylen, said yesterday. It could very well be my last good night's sleep, and I'm not wasting it on nightmares.

I toss my things on the floor next to the bed. "I remember something our driver said yesterday," I tell Maven. "If we need anything we can call him. Want to see if he has something to take the edge off?"

"Let's do it." I was expecting to see a little more hesitation from her, but she's surprised me many times on this trip.

I search for his number in my notes app. The phone rings twice before Jaylen answers.

"This is Jaylen."

"Hi. This is Blair. You gave me your number yesterday. My friend and I took your Uber."

"Yeah, I remember y'all. Taking me up on my offer?"

"I guess we are." I give him our address, and within twenty minutes, he's knocking at the front door.

I answer it. "Please, come in."

He carries a small drawstring backpack and empties its contents onto the coffee table. We stand on the other side across from him while he sits on the sofa. There's multiple types of weed in little clear, plastic bags with the type of strain written on them.

I can't lie and say that this drug transaction doesn't feel a little weird. It's out of character for both of us. There's recreational dispensaries in New York, but not here and not in Georgia either. What we're doing is totally illegal, but it's not the first illegal thing we've done today.

"Which one do you recommend?" I ask Jaylen.

"If you want a long high that gives you energy and euphoria, this one." He points to a bag labeled, *Durban Poison*. "If you want to just chill, this one." He holds up another.

"We'll take both." I hand him the money and we're left to our own devices.

As soon as he leaves, I turn on some music and light our joints. Sinking back into the bed, I lift mine. "Cheers."

Maven taps hers to mine, and we take soft inhales that turn deeper. No coughing fits this time.

"So this is what it's like, huh?" she says next to me. "I fear I've been missing out." Maven takes another long drag and sprawls out her limbs.

I fall deeper into my pillow while a song from *The Killers* plays. The lyrics stand out like they never have before, but it makes me giggle. Killers—if only we could be—our futures would be so different.

Chapter 14

Starve

The light peeking through the curtains wakes me from the best sleep I've had in a while. I check the alarm clock on the bedside table to find it's 11:00am and our last day with souls, or our sanity. I try not to think about it too logically. Anyhow, time is ticking away so I turn back over to nudge Maven awake, whose mouth is wide open with drool all over her pillow. Part of me wants to take a picture of her, but she would scold me for it. Maybe I will, it could be the last picture I take of her.

There's so many possibilities for what lies ahead. Sasha could take away everything I care about until I have nothing left, or she could infect my mind like a parasite until I ultimately find my way to that hallway all by myself.

Go away thoughts, you're not wanted.

I pick up my phone from the night-stand and open my camera. Only, my eyes are drawn to the sight of the little box in the bottom left corner of the screen. A photo I don't remember taking. *What the hell?*

I click on it to see the evil, bitch-demon took photos of both of us while we were sleeping. This lunatic is taking selfies with us in the background, lights out, while our mouths are open, looking a total mess. The camera flash does not suit me. *Is she throwing up a peace sign?* On the other hand, Sasha doesn't look like a mess. I can tell she's being fed, how it revives her. *Do demons sleep?* Probably not. *How does she keep her hair so perfect?* Okay these thoughts aren't welcome either. I lock the screen, deciding I won't take Maven's photo.

I go to delete it. My finger hovers over the button, over Sasha's wide and sharp smile, bearing her pearly whites that are probably sharp as daggers in true form. She is beautiful though with her unnaturally amber-colored eyes. Unlike the crazed look I saw in them before, I see something else. Demons are supposed to be gnarled and nightmar-ish—bald with skin falling off the bone, a voice that makes every hair on your body stand at attention and gapes for eyes.

I saw the void eyes and unnatural snarl flash before me once, it was long enough to know it exists. Demons are great deceivers, I know that. No matter how she appears, like a siren whose hum I can't escape, I know Sasha's true intention. She can sugar-coat it, steal her beauty, slink around in her heels, but I know what she is.

I erase the photo without a second thought.

Maven stirs awake. "Mmm, what time is it?"

"A little past eleven."

"No time to waste, let's get up." She yawns.

"For what?"

She heads for the bathroom. "To go out with a bang. I have some plans for a change." She arches a brow over her shoulder.

"Okay. I guess I'm in the passenger seat today."

It took this for Maven to reclaim her independence. It's a version of her I haven't seen in a long time—the woman who decides to stand up after being cast aside for years, after having her autonomy taken away and fitting into the mold that's expected of her. I only wish I had longer to be with this version.

After we're freshly showered, I sit on the bed to do my makeup while Maven does the same at the vanity across the room. "So what's the first stop?" I ask.

She dabs a light pink blush on the apples of her cheeks. "We're going to eat lunch at the fanciest restaurant in town, then see what trouble finds us."

"Sounds like a plan." Trouble seems to have a tracker on us, so that should be no issue.

"I'm honestly kind of surprised Sasha hasn't shown up since the park," Maven says.

I pause, putting a swipe of concealer under my eyes. "Yeah. Me too."

I'm not telling her about the surprise visit captured on my phone's camera. But I am just as surprised that Sasha hasn't taunted us for the final sacrifice. I thought she would make life as difficult as she threatened, but instead she's ghosting us and taking selfies while we sleep? I'm not going to count myself so lucky because we still have until the stroke of midnight for worse to come to worst.

Either way she still wins, so she doesn't really need the last sacrifice to get what she wants. Maybe that's why she's not going off the deep end because both outcomes are in her favor. If we kill, she's full; if we don't, she's still full and gets to add me to her collection.

It was always a losing game, I realize.

"Forget her," Maven says. "Actually, *fuck her*. In spite of the vile thing, we're going to enjoy this day." She's looking in the mirror, telling this to herself, not me. It's kind of uncanny, but I get it. She practices a smile.

Putting her hands flat on the tabletop, her false smile falls away and her head hangs as her shoulders tremble.

I rush over and wrap my arms around her. "No crying. I've got you."

She wipes away what tears escaped and offers a struggling smile. "I wish I was more like you."

I hug her tighter. "No you don't. There's only one Mave and I wouldn't trade her for anything."

"You've always done what you wanted with your life. You never held back."

"No. I've always taken what I wanted, but pushed away what I probably needed. You have Junior to show for it though."

She shakes her head. "I don't want to talk about him."

I take a step back. "I'm sorry."

"But if I'm proud of anything I've done, it's raising him." She scrunches her nose, pushing away tears, then grabs the powder brush to touch up her makeup. "I don't know why I allowed myself to stay so unhappy for so long."

"We can't change the past, we can only live for today," I tell her. I got that from a therapist I went to once, who I then ghosted right after. Look at me, regurgitating some inspiration. We could both use it.

"You're right," she says. "And I agree, no more tears. If I cry today, slap me."

"I'm not slapping you."

She stands up to face me and before I could predict her movement, she rears her hand back, sending a hot flash across my cheek. "What the fuck, Mave?" I laugh, holding my hand up to my stinging cheek.

"There, it's out of the way. Now when you need to, you won't feel so bad about doing it. We both know I'm a crier and I won't spend any part of today giving her any more of my misery. She can starve."

I rub my cheek. "Deal."

Staff escort us to a table where a single rose stem is placed in the middle of a white table cloth. There's large paintings of who I assume to be the founders on the wall, while large crystal chandeliers scatter across the ceiling.

I didn't pack a fancy dress for fine dining, but since Mave over-packs, I was able to snag one of hers; in a style I would normally never wear. I will say, the green shade compliments the copper in my eyes. It has capped sleeves and cinches snug on the bodice, opening up the neckline with two strings falling loosely—it reminds me of one of those dresses the maiden wears in a romance, but a modern version. The back is open, with two strings running horizontally. Maven wears a yellow-and-white patterned maxi dress, with small white ropes for straps. It enhances the gold in her hair, which falls loosely around her shoulders.

We order lunch and three rounds of cocktails, devouring it all in a very unladylike fashion. The smooth sounds from the jazz band and the taste of crab cakes with a side of gumbo makes me forget about the looming strike of midnight, where we'll dance into oblivion.

The band moves on to a more upbeat selection. I grab Maven's hand. "Come on."

Pulling her to the empty space in front of the band, there are no thoughts, no feelings other than enjoyment. People are meant to dance here, though no one else is doing so. We spin and sway to the sounds of trumpet and jubilee, laughing at ourselves and one another. Dancing in front of a live band during lunch is something I've never done, but something I would recommend.

We've all sat in a restaurant where a band has played, while secretly wanting to dance, but never did because the focus would be on us. Dancing in a nightclub is safe since bodies are indiscernible and no one really remembers, but to dance in an empty, public space? More people would do it if they knew how it felt.

My stomach needs settling and there's so much more left to do, so we pay our bill. "What's next on the agenda, boss?" I ask Maven.

"We're getting our palms read!"

"Nooo," I trail out. "I don't think we have the best of luck with psychics."

"Come on. It has nothing to do with any of this shit we're in. That other woman was obviously the real deal. She was probably a Rootworker. These people at this place I want to go are just for fun. "She pouts her bottom lip out. "It's on my bucket list."

I let out a long sigh. "Well, since we're ticking off bucket lists, I can't deny it of you, so I guess let's go get our palms read."

She claps her hands together, with an ear-grinning smile.

"Any more bucket list to dos I should know about?" I ask.

"Yes. But one thing at a time," she says with a mischievous glint in her eye.

"Are you going to get me in trouble?"

It was always the opposite in our teen years and even past then, when I was the one pulling Mave along with me for some well-deserved fun. Though the mess we've gotten into is because of *my* bad idea involving a Ouija board, she seems to be returning the favor by pulling me along.

At a sloppily pace, we make our way to a psychic shop a few streets down from the restaurant. Above the door, a sign shaped like a tea-cup reads *Crescent City Tea and Psychic Readings*. We open the door and a bell overhead jingles. The walls are filled with shelves of various teas and tarot card decks, among other trinkets. The shop is bright, the floors an aged hardwood like many of the other shops in this part of town. The smell of fruity meeting floral steeped tea fills the air—an improvement from the obnoxious incense at the previous place.

"Welcome, loves," says a young girl at the front desk.

"Hi. We'd like to get two palm readings done if possible," Maven says.

"Definitely possible." She smiles. "What are your names?"

"Maven and Blair."

"Great. Take a seat at one of our cafe tables, pick a tea if you'd like, and your reader will be with you shortly."

I pull one of the lightweight chairs from the circular table with zodiac signs strewn across it in a chart. I point to my zodiac. "Do I exude Aries energy or is it a sham?"

"Oh, total Aries, always have been."

"I don't even know what that means, but I'll take it."

A voice answers from behind us. "Strong-willed, ambitious, impulsive, decided, passionate for the ones you love."

It's a woman with small, long braids trailing down her shoulders and back. She looks similar to the woman at the front desk in the face. It must be a family business.

She extends her hand to Maven and I. "Davina."

I shake it first, and Maven follows. "I'll be doing your reading today," Davina announces.

"I think you kind of already read her," Maven admits.

Davina laughs. "Funny how those things tend to be more accurate than we expect, isn't it? Follow me back, ladies, and we can get started."

We follow her down a long hallway with wooden sliding doors along each side. She slides one open near the end of the hallway, welcoming us to a small room. There's a red, spiral-corded phone on the wall, and a small table centering the room with a dark table cloth patterned in stars creating constellations. A stack of business cards is pushed off to the side, *Davina Delacroix, psychic*. I take one. We all sit comfortably as she offers us some hand sanitizer. Maven helps herself to the bottle and I take some too. It's the best smelling hand sanitizer I've ever used. They must have made it in house with herbs or something special.

"This will give us a clean slate," Davina says. "There's a lot of things out there attaching themselves to us that don't belong."

I scoff. "Isn't that the truth."

I don't know if she's being cryptically metaphorical or cryptically literal. Either way, she's right. I thought this place was one of those shams for tourists. If she ends up being the real deal, this may not go too well.

"So who's first?" Davina asks.

I nudge Maven. "It's on her bucket list. You go."

Davina rests her palms face up on the table, bracelets clanking as she does so. Maven places her hands within them. Davina overturns Maven's hands, inspecting both sides.

She then runs her finger across the lines in each of her palms. "Are you right-handed or left-handed, love?"

"Right," says Maven.

Davina looks over them for a moment. "Your mound of Venus is strong on your left hand and softer on your right." Tracing the muscle below the thumb, she points. "This could mean you're naturally attuned to your sexuality, romance, and indulgence, but these things haven't been actualized in your life. You've been held back."

"Oh. I could see that."

Davina perks up the edge of her mouth. "Palmistry doesn't mean our fates are set in stone; it can just help us understand what we make of what we're given." She moves on to another line in the middle of her right palm. "Your head line is broken on your right. You may be having a monumental breakthrough." Davina looks back and forth between both hands to compare. "And your life line on your left is longer than your right." She traces near her thumb as Maven inspects the lines with her.

Great. A short life line, that's just what we needed a reminder of. I'm beginning to believe this was in fact not a good idea.

"The length of your lifeline dictates others' influence on your path, not how long you'll live," Davina informs. Okay, my interest has peaked. She continues. "This could mean you're stepping into your autonomy and independence."

Well, I could have told Maven all that. It is a little unnerving that she did, though. I have a new trust in the supernatural after the past few days. It's clear demons are real, but are witches, too? Madam Clemence seemed to work with nature—herbs and crystals. But psychic abilities are a power from something else, either within or bestowed.

"So how long have you been doing this?" I ask.

Davina looks up from Maven's palms with a soft smile. "All my life. I was born into it, most of my family are what you could call practitioners."

"Interesting. So you do more than just palmistry, then?"

We share a look that, in some way, suggests we both know the real answer. "I practice with multiple modalities of mysticism," she says.

She addresses Maven now. "Can I tell you something that's not on your palm?"

Maven's eyes widen a little, as do mine. "Sure," Maven says softly.

Davina looks between us both with an endearing smile, like she's about to impart some helpful wisdom upon us. "Sometimes we find ourselves in unsavory situations, but don't be scared of what you don't understand. The bad guys don't always have ill intentions."

I stand, scooting my chair back behind me and Maven pulls her hands from Davina's grip, but she holds them firmly in place. "Do what she asks," Davina pleads to Maven.

"Let me go!" Maven raises her voice and Davina draws her hands back, realizing she overstepped.

"Who are you?" My voice cracks. "Do you know her—Sasha?"

"Does that even matter?" she asks. "What matters is who you are." Davina looks at me with an unnerving intensity as Maven's body collides with mine. *"Dead or alive?"*

Chapter 15

Weirder Things

"At least we didn't have to pay," Maven comments. We're shoulder to shoulder, sitting on the edge of the sidewalk in our fancy dresses.

I want to kick my constricting shoes off. This day is supposed to go how we want, not like this—not with a reminder at every corner. Sasha promised not to bother us anymore now that we've made our decision and she's held up that promise so far.

I shouldn't be wearing shoes that are rubbing a blister onto my heel. I kick them off and toss them next to the nearest trash can within throwing distance.

"What are you doing?" Maven asks.

"What I want, remember? They were uncomfortable."

"Well, mine are too, but I'm not going barefoot around here. This is the last place you should be going barefoot. You'll get a fungus, or a gashed, infected wound."

"Thanks for informing me. What happened to no judgment?"

She raises her hands. "I'm not judging you, I'm just looking out for your best interest."

If she was looking out for my best interest, she would have let me kill that woman rotting away in her hospital bed, but I keep that to myself.

"Any more bucket lists you need to put a check mark next to?" I ask her. "Because I'm all for it, but it seems we attract all the crazies."

"Yeah, it does seem that way, doesn't it?" She rises to her feet, still in her heels, and offers a helping hand out to me. "Let's go get drunk."

"Say no more. I guess I need my shoes for that." I go pick up the scuffed heels from the trash.

The closest bar that didn't look like utter hopelessness happened to not be so far. The neighborhood is basically dripping in them, but this one has a welcoming energy to it. Hopefully this place won't be an illusion. The windows are tinted, the air conditioner is on the perfect setting, and there's faint jazz music playing over speakers.

We choose a cozy corner booth at the far end, away from the door, even though the seating options are endless on account that there's hardly anyone else here. The seat of the booth we're in is made from a rich leather with a tufted back, and the table is polished wood. It's nicer compared to the other pit stop bars, and has an expensive, yet, toned-down quality to it. There are no pool tables or darts, just tables, a bar, and a stage, along with some private rooms in the back, partially shaded by dark green velvet curtains.

I scan over the drink menu on the table. "They have absinthe."

Maven faintly gasps. "That's actually on my bucket list."

I plant my head on the table, with a stifled laugh. "Of course it is."

"What? Not all of us have the opportunity to go to fancy bars and try things."

I raise my head from the smooth, cold tabletop. "Actually, it would be a first for both of us. Never had it."

"Are you saying you're popping a cherry with me today?" She grins. "An absinthe cherry?"

"I am."

A bartender comes over. "What can I get you two ladies?"

"We'll take a few absinthe drinks," I say. "Let's try your Corpse Reviver, Absinthe Sour and...what else, Mave?"

"What's your strongest one?" she asks.

Footsteps echo from behind Maven, then stop where the corner of the wall obstructs my vision. Past the wall is the far end of the bar, where private rooms extend. "That would be the Corpse Reviver," says an interesting voice.

"M—Mr. Bathory," the bartender stammers. "Yes. Corpse Reviver is quite strong. Would you like waters as well?"

Mr. Bathory answers for us, whom I still can't see from my position. What a prick. Another man inserting himself when not asked. "Yes. Add water for the ladies. And the bill is on me."

Maven and I both roll our eyes at the comment. Great. Now he's paying for our drinks and probably thinks we owe him something in return. He probably spends a portion of his paycheck buying women drinks with the hopes of getting lucky by sparing twenty dollars and his affections. The bartender goes to prepare our drinks while the illusive Mr. Bathory steps around the corner, allowing me to put a face to the very formal name.

My brows bunch and I've lost my breath. Holy shit I was wrong. "Mikhaylov Bathory," he offers his name to me with an upturned hand.

I've changed my mind. He can order my food and pay the bill, and I don't care what he expects in return because I think I may give it to him.

"Blair Brooks." I rest my hand on his and he brings it to his lips.

If I were looking at Maven, she would probably have an expression that would suggest I've body-hopped, that the person she's sitting across from is not her best friend because her best friend doesn't get awestruck by anyone, let alone become a puddle.

He's tall with sandy hair that reaches his ears in soft waves, and wide shoulders that have just the right amount of muscle which definitely require exercise, but not all his devotion. He has a softness in his cheeks, though it's balanced with hard lines of a strong brow and Roman nose. His jaw is covered in stubble and his eyes are the most delicious hazel. All these details I scan in our quick introduction because it feels like time has stopped when his gaze locks with mine.

"And you are?" He turns his attention to Maven, while still holding my hand in his, of which adorns a couple of prominent rings.

"Maven," she says.

He nods and takes one step back. "Would you two like to join my friends and I in our private room? Just good conversation and drinks."

I'm trying to place his accent, but I can't.

"I'd love to," I blurt out. Maven sends me an interesting look.

He smiles. "Follow me, then."

I scoot out of the seat, as does Maven. He's within sight, though far enough ahead where he can't hear our whispers. "What do they say around here, *Laissez Les bons temps rouler?*" I suggest to Maven.

"Something like that." She shrugs. "He did kiss your hand, after all."

"He did, right? Just making sure I didn't imagine that."

Mikhaylov waves us over as we grab our purses. He stands like a sentinel, signaling me to where I'm meant to be, wearing a dark blue button-up that's partially open.

"Are you flustered right now?" Maven asks, baffled. "I didn't think that was possible. Don't tell me you find someone who leaves you speechless at the worst moment you could."

"Weirder things have happened," I say.

He pulls the curtain to allow us entry. Inside the small cove there are two other men and one woman seated in a black, velvet booth that curves in the shape of a U. With the curtains closed, the lights are even dimmer. If I didn't know any better, it could be any time of day right now.

We take a seat around the low glass top table, littered with various drinks and an ash tray. Maven seats first, next to the other woman with long, dark hair. She's got a model-esque quality to her. Her hair is pin-straight like silk. She wears a simple, plum spaghetti strap satin dress with a lip stain to match.

Mikhaylov sits next to me, pulling a lit cigarette from the ash-tray and taking a small inhale. "Would you like some?" He holds the cigarette between his fingers.

"Sure." I raise my hand to take the smoke.

An almost undetectable pull tugs at the corner of his mouth. He's staring at mine. He brings the cigarette closer to my lips, tempting me to take it right from his fingers with my mouth. I lose the upper hand because that's exactly what I do. A voice whispers in my head, *The only way to live, is to know that you won't forever*, so I drop my guard, and I look at him while I do it, wrapping my lips around the cigarette tucked between his middle and index finger. And he seems pleased with my confidence to do so.

I know nothing about this man outside of his first name, that he has an accent, and that I'm under his spell.

Reality comes back into frame once the curtain cracks open with a tray poking in. Mikhaylov grabs the drinks from the tray one by one, handing one with green liquid to me.

Acknowledging the presence of the others and catching glances, the other woman offers a slight smile to me. "Veronica," she says with a nod, placing her wine glass on the table.

She's resting into the arms of a man, whom I'm assuming is her partner. His arms are spread out across the back of the booth and is an equal match to her beauty. His jet-black hair, combed back, makes her shade envious.

He extends his hand to each of us. "Adrien. Nice to meet you." He relaxes back into position, eyes fixed on his partner as he kisses her arm. They both have slightly harder accents than Mikhaylov. Ukranian, maybe?

"Blair," I tell them and then take a sip of my drink.

"I must apologize, I gave you my proper name, but you should feel free to call me Mikhayl or as you Americans say it, Michael."

The way he says it in the American way feels foreign on his tongue. "Mikhayl works just fine for me," I tell him.

He smirks, settling into the cushion, an arm behind me. "Do you know the meaning of your name, Blair?"

"Can't say that I've been interested enough to look it up."

He studies me, taking another drag on his cigarette then putting it back into the tray. "It means battlefield. Do you think our names tell us who we are, or we are the makers of our name?"

I lift a brow, taking another drink. "Maybe both. And how do I know you're not making that up, or do you have another Blair in your life?"

"I don't. Some things I just know." He says it with a crooked, teasing grin.

I narrow my eyes at this gorgeous, yet mysterious man and pull up a search engine to prove him wrong. Except I can't, he's right, it does mean battlefield. "Huh. Cultured, are you?"

He extends his arm behind me. "You could say I am."

"Speaking of cultured, I have to ask, your accent—where are you from?"

"Where am *I* from or where is my *accent* from?" he teases.

"I guess your accent," I say, with a short laugh.

"All over, but mostly Southeastern Europe."

"Yet you live here?" I place my glass on the low table and take the lit cigarette from the tray.

"I do. And you, Blair Brooks?"

"It's not important." I blow a small stream of smoke downward.

"No? Where you're from and where you live are not important, why?"

"I'm floating at the moment. Where I go next is up for debate."

He licks his lips. "Well then I should be glad you made this stop."

I don't know what I did to fall into this luck, but thank you to whoever is responsible for this man's fascination with me. *Why me?*

I cross my legs, my knees pointed in his direction. "You say that to all the ladies that come in here, don't you?"

A voice from across says, "He doesn't, actually." This voice carries the same dialect as Mikhayl's. "He is choosy with the women he takes as company."

"That's well enough," says Mikhayl. "Excuse my brother."

"Alek," he introduces himself as he chews on a toothpick. "Maven and I have become acquainted, though it looks as if you and my brother have been lost in your own conversation." Uncharacteristically that brings heat to my cheeks.

"Matter of fact," Veronica says in her smooth voice to Maven, "switch places with us, love, we are only in the way." She and Adrien slide over as Maven moves past them to become better acquainted with Alek.

Alek is similar in appearance to Mikhayl in the face, but looks slightly younger. Alek's hair is a deeper shade of brown and, while tall and handsome, like his brother, he's leaner and has a quality that feels more dangerous. Maybe it's the way he carries himself, the silver chain hanging on his neck or the scar in his brow. Despite the contrast of the two, he seems sweet on Maven. He breaks the pick in two, tossing it on the table and fixates on her with a pleasantry that wasn't there before.

Who are these people? I know now is not the time for questions; it's a time for indulgence and I like this crowd, so I'm not going to ruin it by prodding.

Shit. I snatch up my purse, finding my ring at the bottom, along with Maven's. Sasha made a promise not to bother us, but I can't really trust a demon now, can I? I don't want her showing up and crashing our party, so I slip on my ring and slide Maven's across the table.

"Accessorizing?" Alek asks.

"It's a long story," Maven tells him, as she puts hers on, too. "We got these as a good luck charm and forgot to put them back on."

He takes her hand, inspecting it, likely an excuse to just touch her. "Looks like you don't need it," he says. "You're here with me, are you not?"

My attention turns away from them and back to the man next to me with his arm still wrapped behind me but not touching me.

"It is a nice ring," Mikhayl says, "but not nearly as beautiful and interesting as you."

"You think I'm beautiful or do you just want a nice night with a tourist you'll likely never see again?" I don't know why I'm asking, because I would be fine with either, but I suppose I've always flirted by teasing.

"I could have a nice night in a multitude of ways. I think you're exquisite."

I fix my eyes on his. "The way you speak, it's—"

"Uncommon?" he asks.

"Yes. Uncommon."

He leans closer, bringing his arm resting on the sofa to my shoulder and enveloping me with it. "I like uncommon, don't you?"

It does something to me—the way he looks, the way he speaks and compliments me whether it's true or false. "I do now," I admit.

Taking my chin in between his fingers, he brings his lips closer to mine, brushing his soft stubble against my face, kissing me lightly at first, then deeply, only for a moment. We weren't making out in front of everyone else, but it did feel a little more passionate than what others were meant to lay witness to.

"I was right. You are exquisite," he whispers in my ear.

I look across to see Maven and Alek getting more comfortable, his hand on her thigh. The other two are just as lost in one another as they were when we came in.

Mikhayl grabs his glass of whiskey and finishes it, I do the same. "Should we go back to Maison De Jardins?" He seems to ask his friends. He looks down at me and holds out a hand. "You're coming, are you not?"

"What is Maison De Jardins?"

"My home." His hand hovers, waiting for me to cling to it or deny it. I look over to Maven and she shrugs.

I grab it.

"Let's go, then. The sun is just setting; it will be a fun night." He winks at me. "I promise. I won't disappoint you in making this stop during your float along."

Chapter 16

Warrior

We took Mikhayl's huge pitch-black escalade with matching tinted windows. I assume you need that level of tint come Louisiana's summer heat or he's some high-profile person I'm unaware of. His house sure matches his choice in transportation—obscure—and making me wonder further, *who the hell is this man?* Alas, it's not a night for questions.

The home's white exterior is lit by the remaining cast of indirect sun, diffusing a faint orange glow. With the way I'm feeling right now, the house looks almost incandescent, radiating from within. Standing behind a short iron fence is the grand Italianate-style mansion, nearly fifty times bigger than my apartment. It has three strong columns that stand at the face of the home on both the upper and lower levels. The second story opens up to a balcony viewing the street, with another balcony on the right side of the structure, which I'm sure is facing a view of the private garden he spoke of. I'm not sure exactly what waits for me on the other side of the gate at this beautiful monstrosity, but I'm about to find out.

He opens the front gate, and we flood in behind, all six of us. Stepping through the tall door, I'm transcended back in time. The wooden floor is lacquered, sending reflections across it. The white walls are contrasted with intricate trim, doorways, and wainscoting paneling that are stained so dark it nearly looks black. Adding to the elegance in the entryway are candled sconces hanging on either wall and lighting it in a beautiful dim glow, but what really draws my attention is the warping staircase that curves with a ribbon of red running down the center.

Grand, the entire place commands attention. The black meeting with the red, the candles, the history, it's rich in Gothic detail—the most beautiful home I've ever seen and I've only just walked through the front door.

"You live here?" I ask Mikhayl as he sits his keys on a small table next to the stairs. I'm in awe looking up and around, my head craning to witness the expanse.

"I do, yes." He says it so nonchalantly, like it's no big feat to have a place like this.

The others go ahead into a room past the stairs, as if they've seen this place a million times and it's nothing impressive. He offers his hand to me once more and I take it once again.

He brings us to an oblong-shaped room, with green wallpaper and red curtains that stretch to the floor. A fireplace is lit, the smooth white stone surrounding it extends up the wall with an emblem carved into the overmantle.

"Is this the ballroom? Or was it at one point?" I ask.

"Still is," Mikhayl returns.

"You have balls here?" I laugh nervously. "Who are you?"

"Not often, but yes." He doesn't answer my last question.

Veronica goes over to a semi-circle shaped alcove with seating, where a globed lighting fixture hovers above. She lights a cigarette and Adrien fits behind the bar counter, like he's at home there. He rolls up his sleeves. "Could I fix you another drink?"

My head is already on a swivel and I don't want to forget my last moments. "I'm good for now, thank you."

He pours a few glasses of red wine. If it weren't for the absinthe, I would think I really was witnessing everything in slow motion because as he pours from the bottle, it appears less viscous—the pour thicker and slower.

Just then, my attention is pulled from the curious wine as I feel a hand on my waist, Mikhayl's hand. He looks undeniable under the gentle glow of the chandelier—under any light source really. His color switching eyes of brown and green focus on me with the most want I've felt in a while as a piano starts playing.

"May I take you for a spin on the dance floor? I'll go easy on you," he says.

"I'm not fragile."

He lowers his head and his voice. "I know you're not."

He takes me without warning and floats across the polished wood with expertise. If I didn't take ballroom dancing classes a few years ago when I had a fling with an instructor, it wouldn't matter. Mikhayl commands our movements, making it easy for any woman in my position.

I look at the ring on my finger resting on his shoulder, thankful to Madam Clemence that an interruption can't be summoned as long as I'm wearing it.

"You're a good dancer," he whispers. He sends me out, then returns me in his arms from a quick spin.

"I know."

There's a slight rumble in his chest. "I rather like you, Blair."

I giggle at his way of expressing things. "I suppose I rather like you, too, Mr. Bathory." This elicits a grin from him, showing a sexy set of white teeth.

I've always enjoyed a nice smile, but I catch a flash of a sharp canine, adding to his appeal. I never thought a pointed tooth would be the thing that does it for me, but for some reason it does. Never having paid much attention to whether mine are pointed or worn down, I graze my tongue across my own teeth.

For a second, I feel guilty for leaving Maven to her own devices but as we glide, I see the one playing the tune we're dancing to, Alek on the keys with Mave in his lap. Looking at him, I wouldn't have thought him capable of harnessing such a gentle harmony in his fingertips, but as I'm aware, looks can be deceiving.

Mikhayl continues to carry us across the floor, and the room fades out. He gently smiles at me and it's pure intoxication. As I stare into his eyes, floating across the mirrored wood, I suddenly feel more drunk than I was before. I only had two absinthe drinks. Well, I hear the effects aren't like your average booze, and I believe it because there's a sense of euphoria that comes with it. There must be some secret ingredient that makes everything seem more attractive, better, brighter.

In the swing of things, my attention is peeled from Mikhayl's gaze by the sound of an off-note piano key. And past Mikhayl's shoulder, the room comes into view again, where I see Veronica's bare back. Her dress is down and she's straddling Adrien, whose arms are gripping her frame as she goes up and down. I gently gasp.

"They're unashamed," Mikhayl says, turning me in the other direction, where I only see him and the fireplace to his back. "Annoyingly so."

"They do that a lot—in front of other people?"

"In private company, yes. I don't judge them, but I prefer the uninterrupted company of my lover and I."

Am I his lover for the night? I swallow the pool of saliva collecting as I drool over him, dreaming of what he could do to me. My dream is interrupted by a clash of piano keys that were once so smooth.

"Seems we're the only ones who may think in such ways," he says.

Oh. She's not just sitting on his lap, they're—*Oh.* The cords strike again. You know what? I'm happy for Mave. She gets to fuck some guy on a piano, whom she barely knows...but I've seen about all I've needed to see. Some things friends should just keep private.

"I think that may be our cue to go elsewhere," I suggest.

"I have just the place I would like to show you."

He leads me through a set of French doors. The peacefulness past the iron gates that no passerby gets to witness takes my breath away. I swivel my head to see it all. Luminescent roses climb against the high windows behind me, like a beautiful virus. It's a well-manicured garden with sculpted hedges and other blooms I can't name.

"Maison des Jardins," he says, walking backwards. "House of Gardens."

"I can see why it takes on the name. My place just goes by *The Apartment*."

The corners of his mouth perk. "And where is this apartment, Lover?"

We walk through trees of wisteria, dripping their purple flowers across and through a structured walkway, creating an arched tunnel. The sun has fully set now, the moon peaking and casting its rays through the ivy in scattered patterns. I follow him through the twist of branches and a beam of light shines on his face. He stops his backward steps, pausing our trail under the blooms.

I contemplate his choice of words. "Lover?"

He runs his hand across the dangling petals, causing a few to cascade at my feet. "Am I not your lover tonight? If only for the night?"

He's too hot, too mysterious, too opportunistic to deny. His face lit by a single stream, is that of the last man I'll ever make love to—I decided that an hour ago. Rugged, yet soft, a capable and confident man. And I imagine he may be the best I'll ever have. He opens his mouth to say something, but I cut him off.

"New York. That's where my apartment is. It was soon to be London, but now I'm not so sure."

I need him to jump my bones because I'm getting in my head again. The carefree lightness that came with the absinthe, and somehow his presence, is starting to wane. The heavy weight slowly rests right back on my chest, knowing this is my last chance at connection, my last time having sex, my last everything. I walk past him a few steps to look at the moon, as it could be my final sight of her, too. Everything is more beautiful, more precious now that I know I'll likely never have it again. She shines her dim glow on the plants, the historic rooftops that rise above the garden wall. The little things have so much more importance. And the stars have never looked more beautiful.

"Mikhayl, I may not wake up tomorrow. So it doesn't really matter if I tell you anything about myself then, does it?"

He puts one hand on my waist and trails it around, facing me. He tilts his head, meeting my vision. "Why would you not wake up tomorrow? I assure you're safe with me. I have no intentions of hurting you. If I gave you that impression, I—"

"You didn't." I look up at him. "Life is short."

He smiles, an odd thing to do in response to that statement. Grabbing my hand, he leads me out of the wisteria hideaway and into the fresh air. Past the walkway is a large fountain. Water flows melodic sounds around the statue of a bare woman standing in the center, holding handfuls of fruit. We go past the fountain, and he looks back at me with another slight smile, as if to make sure I'm good.

There's a small tree, where a stone bench sits before it. He lets go of my hand and takes a seat, observing the tree, then pats his hand down at the empty space next to him, motioning me to take it.

"This is a fig tree," he states.

I lower myself beside him. "It's pretty small. Am I supposed to be more impressed?"

"A fig tree lives a long time, did you know?"

"I didn't."

"They can live up to a hundred years. This one is nearly there."

"Actually impressive," I say. I could think of more impressive things right now but I guess I've set the stage with my gloom instead of sex appeal.

"Some say it was the first fruit in existence," he says. "My point in telling you about the fig tree is to say that not all life is short. It doesn't have to be. Some fruits live and die quickly, others are meant to survive." I turn from the boring tree to him. He reaches a hand up to trace my cheek. "You, lover, Guerriere, are meant to survive."

"How do you know?" I mutter. "You have no idea what I'm dealing with."

He puts a hand on my thigh. "I have a gift. Say I can see into a person—one's character—and I have never met a woman as formidable as you. You are a warrior, a woman meant to wage war on a battlefield of her choosing."

I shake my head. "You couldn't know that, you just met me."

He removes his hand and looks forward to the fig tree. "You don't have to understand it, but it's a gift. Just like one of the many psychics in this city may, I know things. Things that would make you shudder, adjust your world view, things that would tear it apart."

His tone is one of seriousness—one that shouldn't be present with a stranger. He shouldn't be so invested in me, nor should he have so much insight into who he believes I am. But he does, and I would be lying if I said it didn't feel nice; to be seen by another person.

"So who are you, Blair Brooks? What will you choose?" His sly smile returns. "Because I think you'll live up to your name."

It's so simple, to be told you're strong and then carry it with you. I've been told it before but for some reason, when he says it, I actually believe it.

I'm in charge of what happens with my life, from what stays the same to what changes. If I'm staying true to myself and my life is really mine, then what shouldn't I do? And what shouldn't I be allowed to have?

I know who I am. I don't fold under pressure, I adjust.

"I would ask you to elaborate on that skill," I say. "But I don't have time for questions, and I think you said exactly what I needed to hear." I stand up in front of him, slipping off my shoes, but not because I want to feel the grass. "Yes."

"Yes?" he asks.

"Yes you're my lover, for the night." I raise the hem of my dress, removing my panties and toss them somewhere in the garden.

He meets me where I stand, kissing my neck at the lowest part, then trailing his way up to my ear. "Then, like a lover, you'll feel me in your bones and I'll feel you in mine," he whispers.

That's so much better than any line I've heard come from a man's lips before. I can't blame the chills running across my skin on the breeze. My nipples peak through the thin linen, my body begging him to ravage me the way he promises. He grabs my breasts, gently squeezing them while kissing me with utter intention, teasing his tongue across mine. I welcome him with everything I have.

Though I try to distract myself, thoughts flood my mind. It's all happened so fast—the decisions we've made, the hours passed. It doesn't feel fair, but life itself is not fair. What can I do? I'm a warrior, not someone who just lets things happen to her. I want it all. I want this, more of this.

He grabs my thigh pulling it up, bending my leg to trace the curve of my ass with his gentle touch. His grip tightens as he lifts me. I'm so enraptured by him, his body pressed against mine, that in what seemed like mere seconds, we've ended up yards away next to the fountain. He places me on the stone ledge surrounding the large circular base. I gaze up at him as he removes his shirt. There's a deep V leading past the line of his pants, making me more enthralled.

I pull on my sleeves to shed my dress.

"Don't you dare." His voice is like gravel as he bends down. "I'm undressing you slowly. *I'm going to savor you.*"

I lay my hands back down at my sides, resting them on the stone, savoring him myself by not touching him yet.

He unfastens his belt, allowing his body to be on full display. In the low light, he looks like a statue—an equal to the woman of the fountain, smooth and hard. He starts at my top, loosening the strings, letting my chest bathe in the moonlight. He goes onto one knee, pulling my dress down in a gentlemanly but scandalous manner with two hands, exposing my chest even further. I'm burning for him, wishing he would release some of the steam as I sit in wait.

Grabbing the back of my neck, he kisses me before moving down to my perked nipples, artfully placing his lips around one. I arch my back, grabbing a fistful of his honeyed waves. He lifts my dress up ever so slowly, gathering it at my waist, and I groan.

"Impatient, lover?"

"Maybe," I let out.

"Don't be."

He pushes my legs apart, burying his face into me, making me rejoice with every movement, every curl of his tongue as I writhe, gripping more hair in my hands, wanting more and more.

I want to feel him in my bones.

It's an electric charge warming and waiting to spark. He savors me with his tongue, just like he promised, worshiping me until I arrive. His hand comes up to wrap around my neck in a possessive hold, forcing me to look up at the stars. The heat rises with every pass until it comes to the precipice, sending jolts of electricity through every joint, rocking me back. There's a sharp prick on my inner thigh, a hurried pain that comes with it. I instinctively tilt my head down to see what the source is, but his grip on my neck tightens, not allowing me to. The pain quickly dissipates, nothing but pleasure and I happily rest into his hold.

He rises to meet my eyes, wiping his lip with his thumb. "You taste exquisite," he trails out. "Do you want me to fuck you like a lover now?"

My heart races and my breath is jagged. "Please."

Though the best has yet to come, I know I would do anything for a second chance at this day.

Chapter 17

Leaving So Soon

After several out of body experiences and getting dressed in the dark, there's no hiding what happened. I don't think it's a secret what everyone was up to in the past hour, either though. We enter through the French doors to an empty room.

"Where do you think the others are?" I ask.

"Likely upstairs," Mikhayl offers. "Would you like a tour?"

I shrug. "Why not?"

"We'll start down here, then."

He leads us to a neighboring room overlooking the gardens, with a glass wall that curves like a waterfall. Except it's darker in here than outside, leaving much concealed.

"This is the sun-room that overlooks the gardens, which you've already seen."

"I don't know," I coon. "You may have to show me again."

He pulls down on a string, turning on a single light. "Surely, I will show you the gardens once more." He winks. "The glass is tinted. I like to spend time thinking out here. It's the best way to see the beauty of the gardens during the day without getting a sun burn."

"Hmm. A man cognizant of skin health. You're rare."

I scan over the room filled with unique pieces displayed, which are not low taste by any means. These are elevated, timeless. He follows my gaze to a drawing or painting, I'm unsure which, but it looks old. It's hung on the plaster wall and is made in varying shades of the same color, depicting a young woman looking down with a halo emitting from behind her.

"An Angel with Titus' Features," he says.

"It looks ancient."

"It is. The original painting made in the 1650s was lost to the second world war."

I know you're not supposed to touch artwork, so I only move closer. "It looks original," I say. "The printer did amazing with this level of quality. I assume you're an art collector?"

"You could say I am," he admits

"I go to plenty of galleries in New York, but I could never afford what they charge. I have a couple of prints in my apartment."

There's a magnificent white vase standing up on a short stone column and filled with fresh roses. It's tall and has a series of scenes painted in blue, wrapping around its diameter. Birth, child, friends, lovers, old age, and finally, death. With the Grim Reaper being depicted in the last scene, I can't help but wonder if he's real. Do we see him when the time comes and does he look like how we all imagine, cloaked in a large hood with a sharp scythe in hand? Or perhaps, does he take on a kinder appearance?

"Something on your mind?" he asks, as I inspect the vase.

"You could say that."

He combs his fingers through my hair. "I meant what I said. Whatever troubles you, I believe you'll overcome."

I crack a smile, letting out a short chuckle. Not because it's humorous that he says I'll overcome my troubles, but because it's nearly impossible for me to. "Would you believe me if I told you I met a real witch—or I guess psychic is the proper term—today?"

"I would."

"Okay, you said that a little too quickly."

He drops his hand and grins. "Well, this city is full of surprises, creatures that go bump in the night."

"True." I nod. "Would you think I was crazy if I said I've seen one myself, a creature that goes bump?" I'm certain I'll scare him off now.

"Not at all."

"Most men would think me crazy for admitting a thing like that."

"Well, I'm not like most men."

I stare at him for a moment, trying to determine what kind of man he actually is. After a moment, I decide he's something new to me. "No. You're not."

He presses his body to mine. "And you are not most women."

It feels good to be told that, even if this moment between us is fleeting. But his face feels like one I could look at every day and never tire from. His company is comfort and surprise. I envision a night like this on replay, how beautiful that could be.

Even if he really is just a man that just gets his kicks from swooning tourists for a night, only so when they recount their trip they'll remember him, I've fallen for it. He's a professional or like Maven said, I've found the one that leaves me speechless.

A silent tear runs down my cheek.

"What makes you cry?" he says softly.

My nose stings fervently while I grip his arm. "Do you think if I wasn't just passing through, that I'm someone you would see again?"

He cups my cheek. "Time and time again." Our foreheads touch. "But it is no question. You'll come back to me."

My nose wrinkles, fighting back a mess of waterworks. "I'm not just temporary? You really think I'm someone worth something?"

Running his thumbs across my cheeks, he dries my tears then kisses me. "Nothing is temporary in my world," he whispers. "If you weren't worth anything, I never would have approached you in the bar. Cheer up."

My mind fuzzies. His words make me forget about the doom, the hallway filled with Sasha's collections, whatever else it was.

I'm being led up the red ribboned staircase to a second floor with a long hallway, where doorways line each side. The walls and ceiling are covered in red wallpaper, where a row of dimly lit candelabra chandeliers trail down. I feel like I'm on a movie set—actually scratch that, I feel like I'm starring in one. Earlier, it was a horror with no hope for the main character, but now it's an impromptu romance with a promising outcome. The earlier doom weighing on my chest has been seemingly lifted by his command.

One of the doors is open and voices trickle out. We approach the room to see a large, canopied bed with clothes littered across it—Veronica and Maven's doing. She's got Maven out of her yellow dress and into an uncharacteristic but drop-dead-gorgeous slip.

"I've not gotten to style another woman in ages," Veronica says, with a smirk and narrow eyes. "I think this is your color, darling."

Maven's wearing a rich, red slip that reaches her ankles and splits up the thigh. It plunges down the neck with a lace border. And her hair is straight. I don't think I've seen her with hair that straight since high school.

"You have to see her perfume collection, B. It's insane," Maven says, catching me in the doorway.

"Looks like I missed out. You looked amazing before, but I barely recognize you, Mave."

"Yes. She looks sexy more than cute, no?" Veronica looks at me for confirmation.

"Totally." I grin at how seriously she's taken it. "I knew you were under there somewhere," I say to Maven while Mikhayl stands behind me with a kind eye.

"I barely recognize myself either, but I like it," Maven says with a fresh exuberance.

"Take it. It's yours now," Veronica says. "Looks better on you than me." Veronica eyes me down. "Now, you. Come."

"I would do as she says. She can be quite bossy." Mikhayl nods playfully. "I will go check in with Alek and Adrien."

I step into the room adorned with clothes. They pour from a large wardrobe at the end of the bed that's surely from the Victorian era. The headboard reaches up to the ceiling with wonderful carvings in the wood; it fits in here, unlike the vanity which is the only modern thing I've seen so far in this house. Bright lights encase the perimeter of the mirror, the same as a Hollywood starlet would have.

"Her color has always been black," Maven offers.

"She knows me best."

Veronica studies me with a watchful eye. "We will see." She goes to the wardrobe and slips a black piece of fabric from its hanger. "Try this."

She seems to be a lover of fine silks and satin. Again I ask myself, *Who are these people? Why do they all live together? And why treat us so?*

Why us? is a loaded question best not to be contended with. Really, the *why* doesn't matter anymore, what matters is the *how* and the *now*. I'll accept the soft silk and put it on my body, I'll take what I want and stop pretending it's out of reach, that some things aren't meant for me—because there's always more to be had. It's a slim possibility I'll have the chance to do all that with however long I have left, but whatever I do have left will be used wisely.

I step into the short satin dress. The front has a slight cowl neck and stops at my thigh, with delicate straps crossing and then draping in a cowl on the back. I look into the floor-to-ceiling antique mirror she has positioned between two massive windows. I'm familiar with expensive tastes, but I'm not familiar with the feeling I have when I look at myself like I do now.

"It's simple, but a statement, I think. You are a slender woman with long legs—simple beauty." Veronica stands behind me and tucks my hair behind my ear, analyzing my reflection, then goes back to the wardrobe to fetch something. She returns with some expensive-looking heeled leather boots. "Try these."

I put them on. They're magnificent, a soft genuine leather with a smooth zipper, stopping just below the knee. I look back in the mirror.

"Black is your color, yes," chimes Veronica.

I feel more than beautiful. I feel empowered. Like Mikhayl said, a warrior meant to wage war on a battlefield of my choosing. I feel alive, more alive than ever, though I'm the closest to death I've ever been.

It's a strange condition to know life so intimately only when death approaches because, only in the face of it, you see all that could and would be.

Veronica waves her hand. "Keep it all. I enjoy dressing you. I will always get more."

I hug her. I'm not a hugger and I don't think she is either because she's hesitant to return soft pats to my back. "Thank you," I say.

"We will go have fashion show now!" Veronica declares.

"I don't know about a fashion show, but I'll show my face."

Following Veronica down the length of the red hallway, I whisper to Maven. "This is how our trip should have begun."

Maven grabs my arm and tries to hide a grin. "I think they're vampires."

I suppress a laugh. "Funny. Don't be ridiculous. Did Adrien happen to over serve you?"

She giggles with a hiccup. "Maybe. But Alek did ask if he could bite me." I choke on my own spit. "I told him maybe on the second date."

"Good idea."

Has she forgotten about the stroke of midnight or just put it out of her mind?

We reach a set of double doors where the men are enjoying a game of poker, but instead of quarters or bills, there's literal gold and silver jewelry—rings, necklaces and even a tiara with precious gems glittering on the betting table.

"A lady doesn't gamble, but I've never been much of a lady. Excuse me, if you will. The jewels are on the winning board tonight," says Veronica.

Mikhayl takes his eyes from the game and looks at me like no one ever has. He looks me over with endearing eyes like he knows me and loves every part that there is—the good and the bad. I know he doesn't truly since we met only hours ago, but I feel like it could be something real, given time—purely by that look alone.

"Exquisite. Will you be staying?" he asks.

Unfortunately, time is something I don't have. "I'd love to, but we actually have somewhere to be." I look to Maven for approval and she nods. "But I've appreciated everything—your hospitality, company, your kind words."

Most of the others follow us down to the entry way.

"Leaving so soon?" Alek asks Maven, rolling a toothpick in his mouth. "Did you not like the way I played music?" He trails a hand down her arm, softly taking her hand, but holding it at a distance as if he wants to pull her along and not let go. "You seemed to prove me otherwise."

"I liked it very much." She blushes. "But we do have...plans before the night is over."

He frowns. "Then come see me tomorrow?"

"I would like to." It's a stab to my chest. She deserves to experience more of this.

Maintaining eye contact, he takes her purse, grabbing her phone from it, and types his number in. "It should always be a lady's choice. Let me know if an angel should want to smile upon a devil once more."

"It was wonderful company," Adrien says, smiling mostly at Maven. The blush to her cheeks grows.

"Come see us again, loves. We don't entertain often," Veronica says, embraced by Adrien.

I get the notification that our ride has arrived. "I will walk you out," Alek says to Maven, flicking his toothpick out into the lawn as they step out into the night.

Mikhayl comes down the stairway, clutching something in his hand. Grabbing both of my hands, he places something with weight in my palm. "For my lover for the night, my warrior. So that you don't forget me. You know where to find me."

It's a hefty silver locket with vines engraved around the edges on a long chain.

I smile. "It's beautiful. And no, I won't forget you, Mikhayl."

"And I you." He kisses my cheek.

He closes the door behind me. Looking back as I walk toward the car, I put the locket around my neck. I crack open the silver heart to see a seed tucked inside, a seed for a fig tree that is meant to survive longer than most.

Chapter 18

Heartbeat

In the room that felt like doom before—where we made a deal to comply with devilish demands and failed—is now only a room and nothing more.

Maven holds her phone as we pose in the outfits we would certainly never be caught dead or alive in before, but now we'll certainly be caught in one of the two. There's just over two hours until midnight.

After seeing how happy she was earlier, hope of a new bright future dangling in front of her, I can't bear to imagine that fate for her.

I'll be breaking my promise of never lying to her. No we won't be going together as she may think.

Sasha never said she wanted both of our souls. There's no reason we should both be dragged down. And though I should feel a sense of doom with that, I feel at peace with it because I know I'm saving Maven.

We look back at the pictures we just took.

"Just like I said before, arson-level. You should post it," I tell Mave.

"You think?"

"Yeah. Tag me in it. What do we have to lose? We look great! Maybe someone will show Matt. He needs to realize what he lost."

She nods slowly. "I agree, he does." She tucks in a smile. "Would it be horrible to say that I have absolutely no emotion attached to ending an eighteen-year-long marriage? I was over it before a man I just met hours ago made me see stars on a piano."

I can't help but chuckle. "Yeah, it seemed like it. No judgment, by the way. I'm glad you saw stars tonight. I did, too. And no it's not horrible, Mave. How could you when Matt gave you no reason to be attached?"

"Alek made me feel more than I've felt in eighteen years," she says. "He made me feel wanted, deserved, like I still have more life left in me. He lit a spark and it's burning, but our candle wick is short, B. That's the miserable part." Her smile turns into a frown.

I wrap my arms around her in a quick and tight bear hug. "Hey don't drop tears, and make me cash in on that slap. We both have more left. It's not the end of the world just yet."

I drop my arms, but she grips her hand on mine. "Do you think it was a mistake? At the hospital?"

I can't believe she just asked me that, though when truly in the face of danger, a person never knows what decision they would make—not until the danger breathing down their neck is no longer a mere threat. And to say we could feel the hot steam exhaling would be an under-statement. It's been burning at our backs the entire day, while we've tried to push it away with drugs, alcohol, and sex.

My brows bunch. "I don't know. If we did go through with it, we wouldn't have known what we do now. What it feels like to live without regret."

"It did feel pretty good to do what I wanted with no fear of judgment, to just be me, the real me," she says.

"The real you." I scrunch my nose. "It was nice to meet her again."

"You, too." She perks her brow. "I saw you with Mikhayl. I haven't seen you like that with someone in a long time, it looked like you really saw him, and like—you let him see you, too."

I smile softly, remembering what it felt like to let my guard down—to be seen and not be scared to do so, to finally stop performing and not just for someone else but for myself. "I did."

So after all, it may be safe to say it was not a mistake to leave that hospital room just as we entered it. Yeah, it would have saved both of us, but we would probably be stuck in the same miserable cycle.

A vibration pulls us apart. The small screen in her hand is lit up with Junior's name. "I don't know if I can do this, Blair."

"It's okay," I tell her. "Just tell him you love him."

Slight panic rises within her. "Why would he be calling me this late? It's probably about the message I sent him."

"I don't know, but if you want to talk to him, you should probably answer it."

"Hey, baby," Maven says holding the phone to her ear. "Is everything okay?" She pauses. "Yeah of course, why? Well, there's a lot of things you don't know, honey." Her forehead wrinkles with discomfort. "It's complicated. Don't worry, okay? Just know I love you, more than anything. You're the most special thing to happen to me." She hangs up the phone. "He knows...about me ending things with his father."

"How did he take it?" I ask.

"He doesn't understand it, of course."

"Of course he doesn't," I tell her. "How could a twenty-one-year-old possibly understand the destruction of something that was built purely for his protection? It's not for him to understand, Mave. He knows you love him. That's all he needs to know."

She rubs her eyes as if to rub away whatever emotion she's feeling. "You know what, where is the other stuff we didn't use last night? Didn't he say it would make you feel euphoria?" She digs around in the bedside table drawer. "Mine is wearing off and I could really use some, how about you?"

I thought I was the one who pushed things away so I wouldn't have to feel them, but if there ever is a time to do that it would be now. Oddly, I want to feel clear-headed for what comes next. "I'm good. You have at it though."

Lights flash through the broken windows of what seems like an abandoned warehouse. I put my phone in my bra. I hold onto it out of habit I suppose, but also it feels wrong to not know how long I have left—even though I've tried my best not to look at the clock today. Maven gladly left her phone back at the house, on a high that I'm slightly jealous of.

"I can feel it inside of me." Maven grins up at the sky, referring to the bass rattling the windows as we enter.

She drags me ahead. There's already a huge crowd and we're in the middle of it. It's a wild sight of glow-in-the-dark body parts scattered in the expanse of the nearly decayed structure, where rusted chains at various lengths hang from the ceiling. I'm not sure if it's a decorative touch and leaning into the theme or if it's left over from whatever operation used to house here. There's a second-story floor with just a walkway and even more people are crowded there. Lights dance from a DJ booth in the back and high energy erupts. Techno music, fueling everyone's movement, echoes so loudly I can feel it like a heartbeat.

I imagine how the quick tempo feels for someone in another state of mind. If I had another opportunity, I may have tried it out. Without drugs, I'm still in a musical trance, my anxiety lowering with every drum, build up, and drop.

We dance like we never have before, jumping up and down on the glitter-littered floor, feeling the heavy bassline in our bloodstream. People bump and ramp up the already bursting energy. I should have done this years ago. I always thought raves were for drug dealers and jobless wanderers, but I was wrong. I was so wrong about so much.

A mashup of an old song we both know by heart comes on in eerie timing. It's a song with a message about living for the night. Is it Sasha sending us a reminder just like she did with the hot tub? If she is, I can't be mad—I fucking love this song. Mave and I sing every word though we can't hear our own voices. We both have lived for the night and I enjoyed every minute of it: the opportunistic wild ride with men we only dream about, knocking down walls, and just saying fuck it why not.

The music rises and I close my eyes, wanting to feel it all. A flood of vibrant euphoria drops heavily on everyone. My body tingles, and for the first time when I think of Sasha and how she showed Maven the wilder side of life, then how she showed me what it's like to live freely and unsheathed, I'm not mad about it.

But I am mad that it took all of this for me to realize I've wasted so much time pretending. Pretending I was okay with what I had has been a defense mechanism. I haven't lived, I've limited myself.

I start crying, dancing out the pain but not pretending any longer. My nose stings and my cheeks dampen. I don't care that I'm surrounded by people, they don't know my story and they probably don't even notice me falling apart.

I open my watery eyes to see another person where Maven was standing. I wipe my eyes with my sleeve and twist in both directions, missing her pink reflective outfit among the masses. People bump into me as I wander through the crowd. How far could she have gotten? The mass of bodies is too large to make decent progress.

There's a little more space on the second floor than below, so I climb up a ladder to my left.

I push farther ahead on the floating walkway toward the middle of the warehouse, so I can scan through the people below. Someone bumps into me, nearly pushing me off. I grip onto the railing, looking down, my body thumping. The lights are too inconsistent, not illuminated well enough to tell one person from another. Everyone is moving too rapidly and packed too tightly to tell who is who. I look at my phone once more, pulling it from the stretchy material of my top.

It's thirty minutes until midnight. Fuck! With everything left to lose, I rip off my ring and toss it below.

And without time to lose, Sasha appears next to me, leaning against the rusted and undependable railing. "Been feeling the real spice of life?" she asks.

I have no time to glare at her or make a rude remark. "What happens at midnight?"

She surveys the people below. "I take *at least* one of your souls." She places a finger under my chin, her nail gently scraping. "Unless you do as promised. And while I may not be able to stick around when you have your precious rocks on, I can still hear."

I accepted my fate already, but I tremble when I say it. "I want you to take me. I'll go easily. Just promise me you'll leave Maven unharmed."

Sasha runs her hand across the rusted metal railing, contemplating my offer. "Are you sure that's what you want?"

"Will you be taking me there"—I struggle to describe my future residence.—"the place you showed us?"

She runs her tongue over her teeth and purses her lips with a clicking sound, looking past me. "You're not *listening*. And you didn't answer my question." Eyes back to me. "Is that what you want?"

"Of course not!" I explode. "What other choice do I have? You've given us an impossible task and you knew it was! Quit playing like I have a choice!" A hot flash surges through my entire body as my fists clench. I take slow steps toward her. "Has anyone ever beat your game?" My nails dig into my palms. "You're a bottom feeder, Misery's Maw." Inching my face closer to hers, I tilt my chin up, eyes rimmed with water. "I wish those words cut deep, but I know they don't. You delight in it, the evil that you are. I can't believe for a *moment* I thought you had a speck of humanity. And you always get what you want, don't you? Well, congratulations."

I back away, having said all I want to say for now. There's nothing more to be done, no notion to sway the pendulum of fate. I may be willing to go easily, but that doesn't mean I'll hold my tongue on the way down. I'm done holding back, with everything.

Her expression is unreadable. "You're right, I do get what I want. Not always how I expect, though." The corner of her lip twitches. "But I knew I wanted you when I saw you up there." She reaches for me but I pull away. "And I knew I would have you in the end."

Chills consume me whole while something in my mind shifts. Did anything matter, any of my efforts? This was an innate design: the house, the spirit board, the contract surely no one has yet to fulfill.

She studies me with her gaze. "Do you want to know why I chose you?"

My vision goes blurry as she rushes forward, grabbing my hand. My head spins, the world around me warping. I press my eyes closed to avoid motion sickness, but it's no use. My feet feel as if they've fallen out from under me. I scramble for purchase and open my eyes. Once my vision clears, I realize I'm on two feet and somewhere different, although familiar.

The attic.

Similar to the first night, the room is gently illuminated by the glow of the moon coming through the small window. And Sasha's silhouette stands before it.

I catch my breath, hand on my thundering chest. "What are we doing here?"

"I knew it when I stood right here. I saw it in you, just like I see it in you now."

"What are you talking about?" I shake my head. There's nothing she sees in me, she's playing another mind game.

She laughs. It echoes against the walls. "Don't act like you don't know."

"You've lost me," I say smugly. I'll give her no satisfaction.

"Then I'll spell it out for you," she says. I don't see her silhouette, only the click of her footsteps and the slow creak of the floor boards that come along with it. "You're poison," she seethes. "A deadly nightshade. There's a darkness in you, Blair. It's perfect." The creaks are coming from behind me now, causing me to instinctively swivel around. "I know you thought about it long after, about killing that woman—about killing anyone." Her voice seems to be coming from every corner. I twist my head, backing up into the window, when she whispers in my ear. I freeze. "I know if it was up to you, you would already be rid of me."

I grip the stool of the window at my back. "What do you want, for me to agree with you? To admit that I'm like you in any way?"

"You're more like me than you want to admit." Her voice echoes from every part of the attic.

"Well, it's not going to happen!" I shout. I wait for some smartass comeback but I'm left with silence. "Sasha?"

Downstairs, I look at the time. It's now twenty minutes till, and I need to at least say goodbye. It's not fair for either of us, but I'm ending this on my terms.

The warehouse hosting the rave is ten minutes away. If I find a ride now and tell them to book it, I can hopefully make it there in time. Damn her to where she came for leaving me here. I tap through the app with frantic fingers, finding a driver two minutes away. My legs shake, not knowing if I'll get the chance to say goodbye.

This could all end exactly where it started, in this wretched house. And I flocked to it, like an insect to ripened fruit.

Chapter 19

Tragedy

The driver picked up on my panic and got me here with minutes to spare. I run inside, pushing past people, where the music still rages. Yet again, Maven's body is lost somewhere in the crowd.

"Sasha!" I scream. I know she can hear me—apparently she's always listening.

Dutifully, she appears. I would like to shout at her for leaving me in the dusty attic, but that's a loss of valuable time.

"I know you know where she is," I say. "Tell me. I'm not doing this without her, we're supposed to be together at the end."

I plead to the demon that feeds on nothing but misery. She should be bloated by now.

Her eyes are transfixed, yet amused. "You're kind of cute when you beg. Do it some more."

Tears fall without any notice. "Please, please! I don't know how else to say it, what else do you want from me? Misery? I've given it to you in droves, we both have." I drop to my knees. "My body—my soul—it's already yours. You can have me, I give you permission. Just let me say goodbye."

That consideration she was observing me with turns into something else—contentedness? And she smirks like she knows a secret. "What if I told you I have what I want?"

I choke up. "How? We never gave you the third."

"It's not the time for questions now is it?" She manifests a folded handkerchief in her hand, offering it for me to take.

"What is this?"

"Your weapon." Her eyes grow wild. "Be careful, it's pokey and deadly."

"Weapon?" I hold onto it, not daring to unwrap it.

"You may need a little help to get there in time. Hold on."

She grabs me, wrapping a hand around my center and pulling me toward her body. Sinking into another warped frame of time and space that only lasts a second, but lifts every hair on my body, sending a wave of both energy and sickness, she teleports us to another location. I scatter to plant my feet on the gray asphalt.

"Breathe," she tells me.

I heave over. "I am, but it's worse the third time."

I lift my head once the dizziness flushes out of my system, to see Ty positioning a pair of legs in neon fishnets in the backseat of a car, her body limp. What the woman said in the *Shimmer Shack*, people who slip others drugs, it's him.

Rage builds quickly. I grip the napkin in my hand, squeezing it as I march closer to his back, forgetting that it's sharp and pokey. I stop to unwrap it, my weapon, to reveal a syringe with a mystery solution.

I turn my head to look at Sasha. She crosses her arms and cocks her hip. "Don't you watch any horror movies? This is the part where you make a choice that alters everything."

Ty's backside faces me as he folds the last of Maven into the back-seat. There's no way in Hell I'll let him do this to her, or allow myself to go out with this as my last image. No. I can't go without defending her and any other woman he'll do this to. I may go to Hell either way, but I'd do it happily like this.

I prepare to release my rage, raising my arm high as he slams the car door closed. Once he turns to face me, I shove the needle deep into his neck, pushing in the mystery solution with force. It didn't need much force, the needle drives deep and blood spatters back at me, painting my cheeks.

I look him dead in the eye with no remorse.

He holds the face of every man that has made a woman vengeful, the sanctimonious face of a person who willingly injects misery into her life with great and sick pleasure, a face that takes without permission—a predator.

His superior expression falls away as the drug floods his system. Surprise, betrayal, anger, defeat—it all flashes before him.

"This time, you're the prey," I whisper because it's all the voice I can muster.

"W-what the fuck?" He stammers as I take two steps back.

"I'm killing you and saving us, that's what." I realize it now. It's not the sole reason for why I drive the needle into his neck, but it's the reward for doing so.

He brings his hand to the wound and I wished it was gnarlier than it is. I want to do it over and over again, to cause pain. The want is all here, bubbling under my skin. Whatever humanity remains within me is holding on by a thread, but enough to hold back my desire. His eyes go blank and he drops to the ground. First his knees hit, then the rest follows. I've imagined before what it may feel like to kill someone, a very particular person. As I look at Ty laying there on the ground, dead eyes looking up at me, I imagine *his* face, the monster who scarred me, who took away what wasn't his.

And I smile. Though I smile, there is no happiness. It's always a dangerous thing when a woman laughs in the face of pain. I let the anger, the pain, the resentment leak through my laughter...and then my tears. They're not for him. Emotions I can't name flood my system as I let out a scream that's drowned out by the music. I drop my knees to the ground, scraping them on the rough pavement. I killed a man. And I'm not guilt-ridden about it.

Tears fall, as everything I've pent up for years escapes, my chest torn open and vulnerable.

I hear claps from behind, Sasha's claps. "Well done, I liked the commentary too—very early 2000s heroine."

She extends her hand and I take it, rising to my feet. I look at my phone through blurry eyes. One minute to spare.

"So now what? We're free?" I ask through short breaths.

"Sure." She smiles. "Don't worry about the body, it was Fentanyl—not as yummy as a brute-force murder, but it will look like an overdose."

"Why did you help me?"

"You said I was evil, and you're right, but I'm the sweetest kind of evil you'll ever meet." She steps so close I can smell her. I haven't picked up on her scent so closely before. She smells of smoke and ash, but there's something else—sweet and sugary, like honey on burnt toast. "The bad guys aren't always bad, right?"

"You're pretty bad," I say, inches apart.

"At least tell me I'm a good liar," she whispers, the words tickling my ear.

My heart starts to pound even harder. It's going to rattle right out of my chest. Anticipation builds as I urge myself to inquire on that. "About?"

"I only lied once." She reaches for me, gliding her thumb across my wet cheek as I still, shivers gliding across my body by her touch. "Your greatest tragedy, Blair, was never the death I promised—it was what would have died inside of you had I not promised it." She leans closer. Her lips press against mine as she kisses me softly, slowly. My arms are at my side, but I kiss her back, a forbidden desire—on my part, at least.

Her lips aren't chapped, they're soft. Her breath isn't horrid, it's sweet. Her teeth aren't sharp, and her touch—it isn't deadly. As much of her there is to hate, I think I always saw the parts hidden beneath, the ones she pretends aren't there because of who she's been made to be. It's complicated, two things can be true at once. She's capable of horrible damage, but she also has the ability to free us from it. And I think, in this moment, who she shows up as is not the being she was made to be.

She backs away, holding both sides of my face. "I never wanted it with me, I just wanted a part of me with you."

She drops her hands away then turns. Her black heels echo on the rough pavement as she leaves from me. This can't be the way we say goodbye, could it? I watch her long black hair flow in the breeze like a beautiful nightmare as she walks away from me.

"Where are you going?" I yell. "Back to the board or did you lie about that, too?"

Spinning to face me, she grins with that wide Cheshire Cat smile, but now it looks less creepy. "No. Not turning in the keys just yet. My hunger is satiated for now, thanks to you. I may go to a department store first—or the beach, who knows." She fades further from my vision and into darkness with every step.

Her absence feels unusual, final. I question if I'm better off having known her or if she really was an ugly thing we barely survived.

"Goodbye," I mutter, for good measure—though, it's a little late for that.

Chapter 20

The Beach

A gentle stream of air cools the top of my head. There's been some turbulence, but lately it's been a smoother ride. Thank goodness, because I need a drink, and not on account of stress, but because celebration is in order.

"Wake up. I got us martinis."

"What time is it?" Maven asks, barely picking up the window shade.

"Does it matter?"

"Not really." She takes the cup from my hand.

"Cheers," I say, raising my plastic cup.

"Wait. This means something. What are we cheering to?"

She's right. It may be the most important one, one to remember above all the others, and pave the way for something new. "To our new life. To not holding back, and to letting ourselves have what we deserve."

She smiles. "I couldn't have said it any better."

The pilot announces himself over the speaker. "Just letting you all know, we'll be landing at London Heathrow Airport in approximately one hour. Thank you for flying with me and I hope you enjoy your time wherever you're headed. Safe travels or welcome home."

"Ready for this next chapter?" I ask.

"You know I am." She taps her cup to mine. "We can get through anything life throws at us as long as we're together."

It feels surreal how we ended up here, where we never would have otherwise. Life almost feels like it's falling into place now. Like maybe it was fate that led us into that attic, if fate is even a thing. I think it must be. I don't discount things we can't explain anymore. If magic workers and demons are real then maybe fate is, too—hell, maybe even angels and vampires if we're being adventurous.

I thought I turned my phone on silent, but my email notification dings. The rental. "*Write a review for Davina. How was your stay? Think about your experience, their place, and the effort they put into making your stay memorable. What do you want other guests to know?*"

That name. I click on the profile icon. I freeze. Her card lives in my purse, still. I dig through it, finding it crumpled in the bottom. *"Davina Delacroix, psychic."* I study the last name, letting it softly roll off my tongue.

"What's going on up there?" Maven asks.

I hand the card over to her. "Davina. She owns the Airbnb." I show her the picture of the host on the app.

"Oh, my god. It is her! I guess she really did know Sasha after all."

My brows furrow, like it will help me to think. "Her last name. Is it familiar to you?"

Maven, quick and ever observant, says, "Madam Clemence Delacroix. They must be related." She chuffs. "That explains why the mention of a random demon scared her far less than the mention of

Ouija board at the rental. She knew exactly who and what demon we were dealing with. And she knew there was only one way out for us."

"Yeah." I nod.

I'm not entirely sure what's going on in that house, what kind of deal Davina may have struck up, if there was a deal at all, and whether it's intended to help or hurt. Maybe we just got lucky in the way we managed to escape nearly unscathed. Whatever led to our dance with death in the form of heels, long black hair, and lips like honey, I don't ever wish to revisit it.

What I'm going to say in my review is going to take way more time to ponder on than I have left on this flight. Still, I pull up my notes app to begin working on what I might say anyway. Maybe I'll type up a big warning sign, a red flag waving, saying: DON'T STAY HERE! IT'S A TRAP!

"Think about your experience." Well, It was like no other, that's for sure. *Haunting, Deadly, Hellish.* Or I could write about how it was a life-altering trip, that without reserving that pink house with teal shutters and a creepy attic, we wouldn't have made the decision to choose ourselves. I'm not sure if Sasha will be the one to come through the board for the next person who dares to play, but if I knew that for certain I would probably say: *It's not for everyone, but the right person will appreciate what this house has to offer.*

Paros, Greece welcomes us when we step off the ferry. We carry our suitcases down the uneven sidewalk crafted from flat rocks in white cement, worn with age. Each building we pass shares the same stark white marble exterior. The sight is beautiful, a breath of fresh air, and just what we needed after our last trip.

About half a mile down the bumpy trek, we reach our stay. The website called it *An ideal location in the heart of Parikia*. We decided on a hotel this time. The door to our retreat is a bright blue that mirrors the bright sky above and promises relaxation.

"This place is perfect," I tell Mave, bringing my suitcase to a rolling stop. "You're officially in charge of travel plans now."

We're flooded by white and timeless opulence as we enter the hotel. I could get used to traveling this way. Our usual place is nothing spectacular, but it's comfortable. This place, however, is beyond dreamy. I'm confident if we give it some time, Maven will give our home in London her decorator's touch. We moved into a flat there, where we're figuring it out one day at a time. The months have gone by, our lives turned upside down, left, and right, but we landed right where we were meant to be—together and finally happy with what's ahead.

The receptionist greets us. "Welcome. Checking in?"

"We are." Maven gives her our names.

The hostess has a bright smile and speaks with a beautiful accent. "What's the occasion of your stay, if I may ask, any celebrations?"

We look at one another with contemplation. "Just celebrating life," I tell her.

She returns a kind look. "Being alive is, indeed, a special occasion." She hands Maven the room key, and I pamphlets with suggestions on things to do and places to visit.

I haphazardly flip through the brochure on the way to our room. "So, where to first?"

"Anywhere we want, but I'm really feeling the beach," Maven says.

"You know, I could probably spend forever with you and never be sick of it. I don't know where that came from, but my therapist said to just say what I'm feeling in the moment without over-thinking it."

She flashes a wide grin. "Good. Because the feeling is returned. You never know when it may be."

The walk to the beach is beyond scenic on top of being secluded. The carefully paved stone walkway transforms into a lesser developed one, where the sounds of crashing waves grows louder. Chatter from people enjoying their afternoon drinks at cafes fade and are replaced with the lull of the water.

I hear the jingle before I see it—an older man herding a small army of goats on the ridge above us, each one with a small bell around its neck. They happily trudge up the trail, dutifully, like they have a thousand times.

I make note it won't be my last time visiting. London is different, busier, but we're still trying to find our place there, our favorite spots, our community.

Settling on a spot, we lay down our towels. Maven rests next to me, facing the ocean while propped up on two elbows. She wears a red bikini—her new color. I lift my sunglasses to the top of my head, watching a white glimmer from the neighboring towering cliffs reflect onto the ultra-blue water.

Our summer beach escape is no longer a fantasy.

The warm sand radiating through the towel feels better than I imagined it would. I've been to beaches, but not a coastline as spectacular and bare as this one. The sand is fine and sparkles like glass. I grab a fist-full, and let it sift through my fingers like an hourglass. It may not be Australia, but less than a four hour flight from London, plus a short ferry ride, the beaches of Greece serve up a slice of life hospitably.

"I've been texting Alek for the past couple days," Maven says, while applying sunscreen.

I roll over onto my stomach for an even tan, but also because I feel a major headache coming on. I bury my face into the towel in order to avoid the sun. It's the oddest thing; these mini migraines have been coming on quick, causing me to black out for mere seconds. I need to see a doctor when I get back. And here it comes, my vision begins to spot.

I prop my head up with one hand. "Yeah? What's he up to?"

She never did trade information with Mikhayl. I remember the bar, Maison De Jardins, and him foremost. What a snack he was, but I guess I'l let her have him. I've told myself it's good not to mess up a thing that was left on a note so perfect. It's no use choosing a side, good or bad—I've belonged to both. But we still wear his locket. It's a reminder not just of him, but that life is what we make of it, for the both of us.

She's ready to let someone love her for more than just the night. Like the locket, Blair's kept her heart closed, cased in an armor. Not anymore. I've helped her open it up, to let her love and be loved. Myself on the other hand—I'm just glad to be out of that fucking attic, now tied to another. Of course, we may get a little bloody on occasion. I have a particular person in mind once we make our way back to the states. And I'm sure Blair would approve.

"He says he misses me, and that they're throwing a ball next month," Maven says. I guess Mikhayl wasn't lying when he said they actually hosted balls there. She lowers her shades. "Do you think about that night as often as I do?"

"Everyday." I trace the heart shaped pendant on our chest.

She tosses her sunscreen aside and leans her neck back, soaking in the sun. "Should we go?"

I ponder on it. Part of me could think of that city as an omen, but upon further consideration I view it as more of a fresh start, our second chance at living to our full potential.

"What do we have to lose?" I ask Maven. "Tell him we'll be there."

She smiles. "Mikhayl said to tell you that if we come, we'll be leaving the city differently than before—as if we didn't last time."

"Isn't that the truth," I say.

I'd heard somewhere that when you take a girl's trip, you always come back changed somehow; it's one of those stupid sayings that pains me to admit is true. I don't overstay my welcome in this body, I've lived long enough to appreciate the dark silence. But I come out when I please, when I want to play.

"Let's just keep ourselves out of trouble this time, okay?" Maven asks.

"Where would be the fun in that?" I tease.

She grabs my hand. "You ready?"

I slink back into my recess, allowing Blair this moment she's longed for.

My vision clears. Shedding our swimwear at the beach, no bikinis, Maven and I don't hesitate to dive right in. It feels like a baptism of sorts—the water cleansing us of everything bad that ever was and welcoming what will be.

Acknowledgments

First of all, thank you to all of my readers over time who have contributed to my journey and improvement as a writer. Readership is an important thing, and I value it greatly.

Writing a story sometimes comes pouring out of you, and other times takes much planning and building. While, like any other, this story took some building—it very much came pouring out of me. After seeing so many women move through life as martyrs, I wrote a darkly comedic paranormal-thriller that explores the complexities of not only the roles women allow the world to put themselves in, but also about how we respond to and can grow from trauma.

This became a flood of female-friendship and self-discovery. And I let it pour onto the pages in a way that felt authentically me. I was lucky to have my own female friendships and other female writers who supported my journey and cheered me on every step of the way. (You know who you are).

On a personal note, I want to thank my husband for supporting my whims. I don't have a degree in writing, but chose to pursue this passion of storytelling, nonetheless, and you never questioned me. I stayed up many nights practicing my craft and you've encouraged my dream of publishing purely because I believed I could.

Cheers! Now go take that girl's trip you've been dreaming of. Just...don't go in the attic. Or do.

About the Author

Emily is from Louisiana, though she's called many places home over the years. She enjoys spending days outdoors with her family, and survives by her espresso machine and Arizona green teas. Blending the magical and mundane, she hopes to leave readers with something to think about long after they're done reading or simply an escape from our world where magic unfortunately doesn't exist...or does it?

Website: Emilyvalebooks.com

Instagram: @emilyvalebooks

Tiktok: @emilyvalebooks

Substack/Newsletter: @emilyvaleauthor

Book Club Discussion Guide

- What were the main themes or messages of the book?

- How did the main character(s) change or grow throughout the story?

- Most thriller or horror stories have a villain. How did the author portray them? Did you understand their motives or methods and did they have any redeeming qualities?

- Did any scene or line make you laugh out loud?

- What do you believe was the purpose for the supernatural element(s) in the story? Was it merely to advance the plot or was it a metaphor for something else?

- The ambiguity of the ending invites you to reflect and decide for yourself what happens next. What do you think happens to the characters after the novel concludes?